op   3⁵⁰

Dear Reader,

Welcome to the second title in the series of *Great Lakes Romances*_{TM}, historical fiction full of love and adventure, set in bygone days on North America's vast inland waters.

Like *Mackinac*, the first in the series, this book relays the excitement and thrills of a tale skillfully told, but does not contain explicit sex, offensive language, or gratuitous violence.

We invite you to tell us what you would like most to read about in *Great Lakes Romances*_{TM}. For your convenience, we have included a survey form at the back of the book. Please fill it out and send it to us, and be sure to watch for the next book in the series, coming in Spring 1991.

Thank you for being a part of *Great Lakes Romances*_{TM}!

Sincerely,
The Publishers

D1617252

P.S. Author Donna Winters loves to hear from her readers. You can write her at P.O. Box 177, Caledonia, MI 49316.

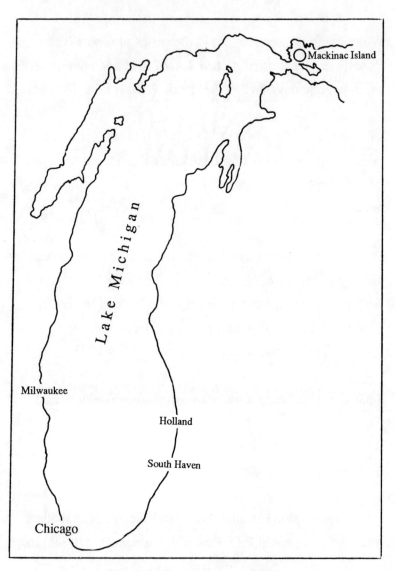

The *Lily Belle's* ports of call.

THE
CAPTAIN
AND THE
WIDOW

DONNA WINTERS

Great Lakes Romances ™

Bigwater Publishing
Caledonia, Michigan

*In memory of Lucy Eddy Winters,
a Victorian lady through and through,
whose image and spirit
have found their way onto the
cover and pages of this book*

♥   ♥   ♥

Notes and Acknowledgments

This novel is a work of fiction. Names, characters, places, and incidents are either the product of the author's imagination or, if real, are used fictitiously.

Ship and port scenes are altered versions of photos from the Appleyard Collection, South Haven, Michigan.

I would like to thank the following people for their help:

Captain Bruce Masse for giving graciously and generously of his time for interviews and tours aboard the *Badger*.

Jay Martin of the Institute for Great Lakes Research for skilled and congenial assistance.

Ken Pott of the Lake Michigan Maritime Museum for opening the Dunkley-Williams records for on-site research.

Pam Chambers for lending books about the Victorian Era from her personal library.

South Haven, Michigan

CHAPTER

1

May 12, 1897

Feeling a bit seasick, Lily Atwood Haynes put her sewing aside and gazed out the window of the parlor deluxe aboard her husband's new steamer, the *Lily Belle*, the only ship in his newly organized Sweetwater Steamship Line. In her wake lay the little port of South Haven on the southwestern Michigan shore. Before her, across the vast expanse of wind-whipped Lake Michigan waters, lay her destination of Milwaukee, some six hours away on the Wisconsin coast. An overnight storm from the northwest had churned up unusually large swells this morning, causing a rocking motion of the ship which seemed to have set Lily's stomach off.

She drew a deep breath and let it out slowly before sitting in the Adam style chair and again taking embroidery in hand. "You've got to concentrate on something besides your tummy, Lily, dear. Mind over matter," she muttered. Once more, she began to count the threads in her cross stitch pattern, then took the next stitch.

Had calmer weather prevailed, Lily would have enjoyed accompanying her husband, Parker, aboard the ship he had begun building a year ago, and decided to name for her last December when they had married. Such an excursion provided a welcome change for two days from a routine in which she had felt lonely, bored, and neglected due to the amount of time Parker spent away from her on ship's business. Her feelings hadn't improved much, she realized, since moving to South Haven from Chicago in April.

Lily begrudged the nasty weather that kept her inside. She would have much preferred walking the sparkling white promenade deck, relishing the cottony abrasion of a gentle lake breeze against her cheeks, and striking up fascinating conversations with other passengers, as she had on a cruise just last week. Today, she waited impatiently in the stateroom for her husband's return.

She remembered his parting words. "I do hope you'll be feeling up to a little luncheon by the time I've finished making my rounds, dear." He had drawn her petite five foot frame up against his well-filled-out six foot one to drop a kiss on her forehead.

Lily caught him by the hand and walked with him to the door, thinking how he looked the perfect image of the vessel's owner in his beige jacket and matching trousers. His tailored shirt with the crisp, white butterfly collar, and the print necktie tied in a large knot marked him as a man of distinction.

"Do be careful, Parker. I hate the thought of your going down into those wretched engine and boiler rooms with all the heavy equipment churning up steam, and the pistons making such a powerful noise you can barely think." On the *Lily Belle's* maiden voyage a month earlier, Parker had insisted on taking Lily below so she could appreciate first hand the seven thousand horsepower being generated. She had not relished the experience.

"Like I've told you many times, love, I grew up on my father's ships. You've nothing to worry about. I was an old hand in the engine room as a lad. Worked my way up from stoker to assistant engineer during summer vacations from Yale. Besides, dressed like this, I have every intention of staying clear of the machinery. I've done my time below decks. Now, I'm glad to leave the dirty work to others, but the crew works more efficiently when you pay them a little attention and give them some praise. It lifts their spirits, makes them feel appreciated."

"Still, I wish you'd stay above decks and let the chief engineer—what's his name—Bates—worry about running things. He and Captain Curtiss seem capable of handling just about anything." Lily's voice, pitched higher than normal for a woman of twenty, her pretty face forming the exaggerated frown she often used to register disapproval, and her well-marked blond eyebrows coming together in a deep vee above her pert nose gave her an engaging, youthful quality.

"They most certainly are competent, or I would never have hired them. Still, I like to see for myself that everything is 'ship shape' as they say. Besides, the crew expects me to drop in whenever I'm aboard. They'd be disappointed if I ignored them this trip. Now don't you worry, love, I'll be back before you miss me."

"Impossible!" The thin veneer of her smile hid the resentment she was feeling. She had seen all too little of him in these early months of their marriage, and on occasion, she had even caught herself sulking over it, but on this trip she was determined to make the best of their time together.

He tweaked her nose. "Well, *almost* before you miss me. Then we'll eat in the dining room, if you're feeling up to it." He named Lily's favorite place on the ship, a room for which she had chosen the mahogany paneling and peach brocade and silk fabrics herself.

"You're doing a perfect imitation of a nervous new ship owner, Parker," she teased. "I'll be glad when you've gotten over the novelty of it all. Now go and check on your crew if you must, but hurry back."

With a grin and a wink, he was gone.

At least an hour had passed since Parker had left to make his rounds. He should have been back by now, Lily thought, remembering the trip last week when she had witnessed his routine. Perhaps he had become involved in a conversation with the men in the pilothouse. He loved to swap stories with them, and might have forgotten the time. She drew the shiny green cotton embroidery floss through the aida cloth, completing another stitch on her design of Mackinac Island, the idyllic resort where she had met him two summers before.

Strange, Lily thought, that the power from the ship's engines had suddenly been cut, their steady vibration reduced to a whispering hum just when the pitching of the vessel seemed more severe. What could possibly require such an action in the middle of the lake, she wondered? She hoped Parker hadn't spent all this time in the engine room and found something amiss. When he stayed longer than a few minutes near the machinery, the odor of oil lingered on his clothing, and the way Lily was feeling, she didn't think she could tolerate the unpleasant smell.

She sighed, set down her embroidery, and stepped to the parlor window. Though she was feeling only slightly improved, she was eager to have Parker back, to go to luncheon with him, if only to nibble crackers while he ate, and then to walk the deck where she could catch a breath of fresh lake air. Though the waters were still plenty choppy, the sun had shown its face. Perhaps the soothing warmth of its rays would make her feel better.

Impatiently, Lily crossed the parlor to the dresser and checked her image in the mirror. Her pixie-like face made her appear younger than twenty. She fussed with a long golden strand that had escaped her Gibson Girl hairstyle, then took up her embroidery again. Determined to overcome her impatience, she began humming to herself as she concentrated on her needlework, drawing the thread through the fabric with equal tension on each stitch.

She had worked for another half hour on her design when a knock sounded on her cabin door. Perhaps Parker, realizing an engine problem would delay his return, had sent a steward with a message. If so, she would ask him to bring a glass of spring water and some common crackers.

Opening the door, she realized her taste for bottled water would have to wait. "Captain Curtiss, I wasn't expecting such a distinguished visitor."

A moment passed before the grim-faced captain spoke, and when he did, he carefully measured his quiet words. "Ma'am, I need to talk to you . . . about Mr. Haynes."

She stepped back, inviting him in. A feeling of foreboding came over her at the somber tone of his voice and the droop of his mustached and bearded mouth.

The captain's broad shoulders filled the doorway as he entered the room. He closed the door gently behind him and leaned against it, appearing more solemn than she had ever seen him. "Please, Mrs. Haynes . . . have a seat." He removed his cap. Eyes downcast, he began turning it in his hands. The tense angle of his jaw was softened only slightly by a closely cropped chestnut beard. Hair to match, lots of it, swept back off his face in neat waves that rippled in an even, carefully groomed fashion. The ruddy tone of his rounded cheeks and grooved forehead attested to his years as a lake sailor who had reached his mid-thirties.

She perched stiffly on the edge of the straight chair and leaned slightly forward, twisting a handkerchief into an ever tighter coil as the silent seconds passed.

11

"You've come to see me about Parker?"

His eyes met hers. He nodded, drawing a breath to speak, but no words came out.

Sensing the captain's difficulty, Lily forced a smile and made a guess as to the reason for his visit. "I know. He's becoming a bother to you with all his checking on the crew—in your pilothouse where he shouldn't be interrupting you and your wheelsman and navigator, down in the engine room where he's probably sending his chief engineer into nervous fits. I'll talk to him about it. I won't even tell him you've come to see me—"

Captain Curtiss shook his head and interrupted. "Th . . . th . . . that's not why I've come, ma'am. Mr. Haynes is . . . was welcome in any part of the ship by every man, officers and crew . . . at any time. We all respected and appreciated . . . his interest in running . . . the best ship in the business." After an abrupt start, the captain spoke so slowly Lily had wanted to finish his sentence for him.

She tilted her head. "Respected? Appreciated?" She gave a sharp laugh. "Your use of past tense makes it sound as if he's been lost overboard, Captain Curtiss."

His head moved from side to side. "N . . . n . . . no, ma'am." His bass voice had quieted to a half whisper. The lines in his forehead deepened and his soft brown eyes seemed to mist over. He pulled up a chair and sat facing her. Setting aside his cap, he enfolded her delicate hands inside his large, weathered ones and looked directly into her puzzled sapphire eyes. "M . . . Mister Haynes has not been lost overboard. What I came to tell you is . . . worse."

CHAPTER 2

May 12, 1897
Cleared South Haven bound for Milwaukee 9:10 in
brisk northwest breeze and six foot swells. Two
hours out, hit rougher water. Parker Haynes killed in
engine room accident. Engines placed on standby
one hour. Arrived Milwaukee 16:35.

At the mahogany desk in the captain's quarters of the
Lily Belle, now snug against her pier in Milwaukee, Hoyt set
aside the leather-bound volume containing the ship's official
records, placing it upright between the anchor-shaped
bookends, two of only a half dozen objects that decorated
his small, sparse quarters aboard the steamer. Unlocking the
top right desk drawer, he removed his personal journal and
laid it open to write a comprehensive account of his day.

He had been setting his thoughts to paper since the age
of twelve. No matter where life had taken him—aboard the
countless Lake Michigan steamers he had served as a crew
member, to the farm in Wisconsin where he spent his winters, to his childhood home in Chicago where his mother had
remained until her death three years back—he had managed
to find a place where he could write about his feelings
whenever they demanded release. For many years, his
quarters had been in the forward cabin with dozens of other
seamen who had but a narrow bunk and a ditty bag to call
their own. By comparison, his captain's suite aboard the
Lily Belle, with its sofa, bed, couch, two chairs, and bathroom, seemed luxuriously roomy.

He turned to the first blank page in his diary and again

took pen in hand. His journal writings, unlike the terse accounts given of ships' passages in official record books, included his most private thoughts, emotions not shared with another living soul, either because he could not voice them due to the struggle against the stammer which always threatened his speech, or because such intimate feelings could not properly be divulged, even to one's closest friend.

Hoyt had long ago learned to take advantage of the purging process of writing about his feelings. The habit had helped him to release his resentments, to come to know himself better, and to understand others and learn compassion. He had taken up the practice when confined at home in Chicago due to allergies and asthma which had kept him too weak to play outdoors with his brothers and the neighbor boys. Those difficult days of his youth were far from his mind this evening, when he began to commit the fabric of his day to paper.

> *May 12, 1897. The worst day of my life.*
>
> *How can words describe the loss of a friend? Only twelve hours have passed. I am numb with shock. I find myself hoping I will awaken and discover today was only a nightmare.*
>
> *I cannot begin to describe my feelings at finding a human body mangled by a rotating crankshaft. The incident would be tragic enough were the man a stranger, but this individual was a friend of many years.*
>
> *Parker Haynes, dead at age thirty. I still cannot comprehend the truth of it. I cannot envision the future without him in it—we have been together on the lakes for so long.*
>
> *I keep asking myself how this accident could have*

14

happened. Parker well knew the dangers of the engine room, but he was ever fascinated by his triple expansion engines.

It was his misfortune to be in the wrong place at the wrong time. Neither he, nor I could know of the rough water ahead that would pitch the Lily Belle *enough to cause oil spillage by the oiler, and Parker's subsequent loss of balance.*

An inner voice tells me all factors were beyond my control, especially Parker's presence in the engine room. He loved his new ship, and her engines most of all. Nothing could keep him away from them.

I spent thirty minutes deciding how to tell his wife she is now a widow, and praying my jaw would not lock into the trembling static mode that would keep me from speaking altogether.

After a fashion, I managed to tell her what happened. Hearing the news, she emptied the contents of her stomach in the toilet. My own stomach had turned several times before going to her.

Mrs. Haynes was a bride of only four months. She has a small, delicate build, too dainty-looking to take care of herself, I think. I suppose she'll return to her family back East.

She asked me if I would cancel her husband's business meetings scheduled for today, which I did.

She says she will retain Parker's stepbrother as superintendent of the Lily Belle. *I didn't let on that I was disappointed in her choice.*

May 21, 1897

I have made a promise to myself to call on Lily Haynes each Tuesday and Friday afternoon, when I

15

make the run from South Haven to Chicago. She has decided not to return East, but to stay in Chicago with a Mrs. Agatha Atwood, her great aunt.

Today was the first of my calls. I went with a sense of dread because of my slow tongue. I needn't have worried. Mrs. Haynes and Mrs. Atwood are easy with words and did not expect me to contribute much to the conversation.

Mrs. Haynes seemed pleased with the five pounds of Murdick's fudge I had arranged to obtain when Mad Jack visited Mackinac Island.

May 25, 1897

Spent a pleasant half-hour this afternoon in conversation with Mrs. Haynes and Mrs. Atwood. Mrs. Haynes asked how the Lily Belle is faring and seemed sincerely interested. I don't know if I should tell her the ship could do better under different management.

Mrs. Atwood was very witty, quoting Benjamin Franklin this afternoon. Upon my leave-taking, Mrs. Haynes made a point of telling me in private that her aunt had enjoyed my visit enormously, and she hoped I would continue to call when my schedule allowed.

July 8, 1897

I am not looking forward to calling on Lily tomorrow. I hate to burden her about the trouble with the Lily Belle, considering the problems she has already been through.

CHAPTER

3

Chicago, July 9, 1897

The heat was again oppressive as it had been for the past several days, and Lily searched her wardrobe for lightweight apparel. She pulled a dark purple linen skirt and subdued silk lavender blouse from her closet and laid them on her bed. Thank goodness, she was not expected to wear mourning while at home. Though she would continue to wear black in public for a long while, she was glad that in these modern times, it was considered a matter of personal choice rather than a requirement.

Since she had been a bride of only four months when widowed, she had no intention of spending eighteen months grieving over her loss. If the truth be known, she had been recovering quite nicely in the two months since the tragedy, helped along in no small part by her disillusionment with the increasingly unhappy marriage in which she had felt trapped and ignored much of the time.

Though Parker Haynes had been fun loving and affectionate when he had courted her, he had become eager to return to Chicago after one week of their month-long European honeymoon, and once stateside, he had lavished his attentions on another woman—his mistress, the *Lily Belle*. Lily had learned a hard fact during the months when the vessel was being fitted out, and Parker's new company, the Sweetwater Steamship Line, was being organized: that the *Lily Belle* of wood and steel would always take precedence over the Lily Belle of flesh and blood.

She had asked herself constantly during her short mar-

17

riage why she had not seen trouble coming, and her conclusion had been simple. Parker was as charismatic as he was dashingly handsome, and she had fallen hard for the image he presented. Beneath the surface, he was driven to prove himself in a man's world. His new business, and this concentration of purpose left little time and energy for a home life.

Of course, she realized the importance of success to Parker. He had left the Haynes Steamship Line, a fleet of railroad car ferries which had been founded by his father and inherited by himself and his stepbrother, Alick, three years ago. Alick had predicted failure for Parker, and said he would be back for his old job within a year. As a matter of pride, Parker had set out to prove Alick wrong, sacrificing nearly every waking moment and ounce of energy in the process.

Parker's answer to Lily's complaints of boredom after the honeymoon while living in the family home they had shared with his stepbrother in Chicago, was to buy her the largest house in South Haven, which was to be the home port of his new company once the shipping season opened, and give her an unlimited decorating budget. Though she tried several times to explain how she felt, Parker simply would not face the fact that what Lily wanted and needed most in her life was time with him, not diversions.

Regardless of the misgivings over her marriage, Lily was delighted with the ship that bore her name. She had even visited Alick Haynes at his dockside office in the Haynes Steamship Line building on two occasions to inquire about the *Lily Belle's* financial status, but had been unable to learn any particulars. Alick had assured her that he had retrieved all of the documents regarding the Sweetwater Steamship Line from Parker's office at their South Haven home, and remarked about her own East Coast family being too wealthy to let her go wanting, then quickly ushered her out. Next time she visited, she would not be brushed off so easily.

According to Captain Curtiss, the *Lily Belle* had seen an increase in traffic each week since she had begun offering weekday passenger and freight service from South Haven to Milwaukee and Chicago, and weekend excursions for Sunday School and civic groups to Holland or Benton Harbor and St. Joe, depending on need. The *Lily Belle* was now operating near capacity. This week, she had run to Milwaukee on special charter taking a load of teachers to the National Education Association convention, along with the *Christopher Columbus*, the *Virginia*, and the *Northwestern*. Parker would have been proud of such a record.

Lily finished hooking the pleated blouse front and fastened her watch pendant around her neck. Captain Curtiss would soon arrive, and she looked forward to his visit. For a man who had dedicated his life to Lake Michigan, he had paid her more sincere attention in the two months of her widowhood than Parker had in the last three months of their marriage!

Descending the stairs, Lily entered the parlor where her elderly aunt, who had been looking pale of late due to the high temperatures, was already sitting in wait for the front bell to ring. Visits from the captain had become a highlight in Agatha Atwood's life, Lily had noticed, and she was glad for the enjoyment her aging relative derived from them. This afternoon, her aunt had more color in her cheeks than in the last two days. She had put on her prettiest mauve dress with the lace-edged collar, and it complimented nicely her white hair and delicate complexion.

She sat on one of a pair of William and Mary chairs,

19

upholstered in her own needlework depicting dusty pink roses. Lily took the one opposite, leaving the brown plush sofa for Hoyt. Amidst the conversation grouping was an oblong walnut table with turned legs and stretchers, its top delicately inlaid with a seaweed design. Here, Agatha's hired woman, Margaret, would serve tea.

"Aunt Agatha, you look absolutely charming on this wretchedly hot afternoon. Captain Curtiss shall soon be asking to take you for a drive down by the water to catch a breeze off the lake," Lily teased.

Though Agatha waved off her niece's compliment, a smile tipped the corners of her mouth. "Now Lily, 'tis you that keeps him coming, and I dare say were it in the least ways proper, he'd have taken you for a drive long before now."

The words were no sooner spoken than the bell sounded, and Margaret announced the captain. Of medium height but heavily built, his neat-fitting navy blue jacket showed his wide chest to good advantage. As he seated himself on the couch, he offered a pleasant smile, but it faded too quickly, Lily noticed.

"I trust you enjoyed a smooth crossing today, Captain Curtiss," Agatha said.

Accustomed to the hesitation that often preceded his response, the women waited patiently for him to organize his words. "Lake weather is fair. Light winds, calm waters, plenty of sun, and cooler temperatures than in the city. Couldn't ask for better."

Lily asked, "With such an excellent report, what is behind the worry lines on your forehead?"

Before he could answer, Margaret had brought in the beverage tray, a dainty fluted silver oval with three crystal glasses filled with ice and lemonade, and already moist with condensation.

The etched Waterford glassware seemed out of place in the captain's large, weathered hands, but he managed the drink nicely as he answered her question. "I see a storm brewing ashore, but I won't burden you with that until we've enjoyed our refreshment."

Though Lily was eager to know more, she managed to quell her curiosity during several minutes of pleasant conversation, waiting until the glasses had been set aside to raise further inquiry.

"Tell me about this storm you see onshore, Captain Curtiss."

He leaned forward, his brown eyes steady on Lily. Since becoming widowed, her face had lost its round, carefree look, trading it for a more oval shape and somber expression. The blue eyes with which she regarded him were troubled, making him regret even more what he must tell her. "I . . . I know you are a very rich lady, Mrs. Haynes, and m . . . maybe this is of no consequence to you . . . but Alick Haynes is embezzling from the revenues of the *Lily Belle*."

Lily's brows shot up. "How did you find out?"

"P . . . Purser Fairfield discovered it. Tuesday, he went to Alick's office looking for records of the *B . . . Belle*—receipts. Alick wasn't there . . . but everything was unlocked. Fairfield came across a second set of books. He didn't have time for an exact accounting . . . but several thousand dollars were m . . . m . . . misappropriated. I've known both men a long time. I trust Fairfield. Alick . . . ?" His head moved slowly from side to side.

"I'm not surprised," Agatha said matter-of-factly. "I've never liked that Alick Haynes, not from the moment I first met him at your wedding, Lily. He's got shifty gray eyes. Can't trust a man with shifty eyes, I always say."

21

Lily had sensed a rivalry between Parker and his step-brother, but that was no cause for such dishonesty on the part of Alick. His cheating enraged her. "After all Parker sacrificed to ensure the success of the *Lily Belle*, I'm not about to let Alick steal one solitary penny. Captain Curtiss, if I may, I'll ride with you to the dock and pay Alick a visit this very day to relieve him of his duties concerning the Sweetwater Steamship Line. I'd sooner run the *Lily Belle* myself, than allow her to be run into the ground by an unscrupulous superintendent." She consulted her watch. "I have just enough time to give him the news before he leaves his office for the weekend."

Within minutes, a hansom cab bearing Lily and the captain jostled toward Alick's office near the Haynes Steamship Line docks, wending its way through the sweltering afternoon heat over brick streets clamoring with the clatter of a horse drawn wagon, the clip-clop of a policeman on his mount, and the calls of a newsboy hawking the evening paper.

Lily hadn't even taken time to change into mourning, but such was the least of her worries. She could only think how resentful she was that Alick had illegally enriched himself by taking advantage of Parker's passing and the risks he had been willing to take.

Looking for a new challenge at age thirty, Parker had taken a substantial loan to build the *Lily Belle*, planning to pay it off within five seasons or less. He had also convinced Alick to lease him dock space, sell him coal for refueling, and provide ticket offices for passengers in his three ports through agreements with the Haynes Steamship Line.

As the cab neared the Rush Street Bridge, where the *Lily Belle* was taking on freight not two hundred feet from

Alick's office, Hoyt cautioned Lily. "I'll go with you to see Alick, ma'am. I don't trust him to remember you're a lady, once you've delivered your b . . . bad news."

"Your concern is greatly appreciated, captain, but I'm not anticipating any trouble." She blotted perspiration from her forehead with a lacy handkerchief, instructed the driver to wait for her, then accepted Hoyt's assistance from the cab.

Knowing confrontation would get her nowhere, Lily entered Alick's spacious office with a sweet smile in place, and words that rolled off her tongue like honey. "Alick, darling, how wonderful you look." She seemingly floated across the room to where the lean, tall figure was rising from his desk, and placed a sisterly kiss on his thin cheek. Hoyt remained silent by the door.

"Lily, to what do I owe this pleasant surprise?" Alick kissed the cheek she offered, then taking her hands in his, held her apart from him. "Out of mourning already, I see. But then, I suppose that's the way of it with you forward thinking young women."

She released her hands from his. "Yes, that's the way of it. And in keeping with my forward thinking, I've decided to relieve you of a huge burden, my dear, kind Alick. I've grown terribly bored with the secluded life of a mourning widow, and rather than wilt away, I've decided to spring ahead to new challenges." She strutted back and forth in front of his cluttered desk, noting her ship's name on several documents that fluttered beneath paperweights in the breeze of Alick's electric fan.

"I've come for the records of the *Lily Belle*. From now on, you'll not have to trouble yourself over her affairs. I'll see to them myself, and save you the effort." Quickly, she began gathering up the papers on his blotter.

"Lily, dear, aren't you overlooking something?" he asked, coming around the desk. The vein at his temple grew more prominent, and his piercing gray eyes narrowed, giving his face a taut look.

"What might that be, Alick?" she asked innocently.

"You don't know the first thing about running a ship," he sneered, reaching for the documents.

She hid them playfully behind her back. "Now, Alick. You underestimate me." Though she tried to mask her apprehension, her voice quavered.

He grabbed her roughly by the wrist, evidently unaware of Hoyt until he stepped forward, hands on hips, feet splayed, challenging Alick with a glaring look.

Begrudgingly, he released Lily. "Yes. I can see that," he said through gritted teeth.

"I'll be out of here just as soon as I've gathered together all the records," Lily quietly stated, moving quickly to jog together the messy stack.

Resignedly, Alick sat again, leaning back to prop his feet on his desk and fan himself with a manila folder while Lily helped herself to leather bound volumes inscribed in gold with *Official Records—Lily Belle*. "You're making a big mistake, Lily. Mark my words."

"*You're* the one who made the big mistake, Alick. Did you really think you could get away with your thievery, or did you just think I was too rich to care?"

In one swift motion, his feet swung down and he stood, leaning across his desk menacingly. "Who told you I was stealing from you?" His sights on Hoyt, he accused, "Curtiss, you're the one who's been filling her head with lies, aren't you?"

Hoyt's tongue pasted itself to the roof of his mouth, and he silently berated himself for his inability to reveal the

24

sordid truth about Alick's character. Of course, Alick had known words would fail him, and as in their youth, was taking full advantage.

Lily gave a haughty laugh. "You must be mad if you think I'd divulge my source. You've got no case against my captain, Alick. If you have any complaints, you take them up with *me*. But of course, you won't have any, because you're guilty, and you know these records will prove it." Arms laden with papers and ledgers, Lily waltzed out of the office.

Hoyt closed the door behind them and relieved Lily of her burden, swinging it beneath one arm. He wanted to tell her how much he admired her spunk. Still, words would not come.

Lily seemed talkative enough for them both. "You see, Captain? I said I wasn't anticipating any trouble. Now, if I can just make some sense of this mess, we might even be able to keep the Sweetwater Steamship Line in business for another week or two."

Forcing his mouth to move, Hoyt offered, "I'll help you."

Lily smiled up at him. "I knew I could count on you, Captain." Stepping outside into the sunshine, Lily noted that the cab driver was waiting where they had left him. She checked the time on her watch necklace. "Well, I'd best get back to Auntie's and see what I've gotten myself into." She shaded her eyes to look again at the ship which bore her name. "With your departure only an hour off, you're probably anxious to return to your duties."

Hoyt nodded, and walked with her to the hansom, realizing that this time, he did not want to leave Lily behind. She was full of spark and spitfire, but Alick Haynes could play mean and nasty, and he hated leaving her in the same town with him.

When they reached the carriage, Lily turned to face him. "Captain, I've just decided, come next Tuesday, I'm going back to South Haven with you. If I'm going to run the Sweetwater Steamship Line, it's time I live my own life in my own home. Besides, Parker's office is set up there, so I might as well make use of it."

Though he mentally applauded Lily's decision, he hated to see her alone in the ten-room Queen Anne home Parker had given her. "Perhaps your aunt will come with you."

Lily stepped into the carriage, pondering the suggestion while Hoyt laid the ship's papers on the seat beside her. When his caring brown eyes met hers, a thoughtful smile was curving her mouth. "Perhaps she will, Captain. I'll see if I can convince her."

His mouth turned up as he nodded approval. Touching the brim of his cap, he said, "Until Tuesday."

"Pleasant sailing, Captain."

By the time Lily let herself in her aunt's front door and locked it behind her, the elderly lady had limped with the aid of her cane from the parlor to the foyer.

"How many arms did Captain Curtiss have to twist to get you those?" she asked pointedly, eyeing Lily's stack of papers and record books.

Lily grinned broadly. "Not a one, Auntie. You know how winsome I can be. I just connyfogled Alick right out of them." She headed toward the office her Uncle Wilbur had kept at the back of the house.

Agatha followed closely behind. "I've never doubted your charms, my dear. They're second only to your tendency to exaggerate."

"You know me too well, Auntie. Actually, Captain

26

Curtiss's intimidating presence saved the day." She set her heavy stack atop the large oak table in the center of the room and began perusing the first document while her aunt opened the many-faceted and pigeon-holed Wooton desk.

Taking out paper, pens, and ink bottle, Agatha laid them on the table and pulled up a chair. Lily looked up from the page, her head moving slowly from side to side. "I haven't the slightest idea what all this means." She handed the paper to her aunt.

Agatha read the masthead. "Hmm. An insurance policy with Johnson & Higgins, the biggest broker in the business."

"It reads like a foreign language. Honestly, Auntie, I don't know what gave me the idea I could run a shipping business." She slumped onto the chair in defeat.

Setting aside the policy, Agatha pulled up a second chair and sat beside her niece. "Now, Lily, this won't be the first time a widow in the Midwest has taken over her husband's business. Mrs. McCormick did a fine job of filling Cyrus's shoes in '84, and when I lost my Wilbur back in '87, I picked up right where he left off. You can do it if you really want to." Agatha jabbed her finger in the air. "'Drive thy business or it will drive thee,' Ben Franklin used to say. 'Diligence is the mother of good luck.' I'll be glad to help you all I can."

Lily took Agatha's hands in hers. "Will you really help me, Auntie? I'd like to move back to South Haven and run the business from there the way Parker did. Will you come with me? *Please?* It will be cooler than in the city."

Agatha squeezed her niece's hands. "You don't have to ask twice, Niece. When do we leave?"

"Next Tuesday, if that's all right."

Agatha again picked up the insurance policy. "I won't let you out of Chicago without me. Now, if you'll please

27

fetch my pince-nez, I'll explain this policy to you. We've got lots to learn before Tuesday comes, and we'd best not waste any more time."

Lily hugged her aunt, and quickly went in search of the glasses.

Agatha Atwood, despite her seventy years, or perhaps because of them, possessed an acute understanding of business functions and legal documents from forty years of helping her late husband successfully run a half dozen entrepreneurial ventures, and ten years of doing it single-handedly as his widow. In no time, she had analyzed the Johnson & Higgins insurance policy.

After a dinner break, Agatha patiently helped her niece make sense of freight contracts and personnel files. At midnight, they agreed to retire and rise early the next morning to resume their work.

By Monday afternoon, Lily and Agatha had finished their study of the papers retrieved from Alick's office, and had begun, with Margaret's help, to pack their belongings for the trip to South Haven. As Lily laid her corsets neatly inside her trunk, she wondered whether she would be wearing them much longer. In the past several weeks she had noticed changes in herself that made her suspect she could be carrying Parker's child. She made a mental note to consult a doctor once she had returned to South Haven.

When Tuesday afternoon arrived, Hoyt came calling in a coach large enough to carry the trunks, and with a coachman strong enough to help load them into the luggage rack on top. Margaret had welcomed the suggestion that she come to South Haven and continue in service at the Haynes home, while Agatha's gardener agreed to oversee her property in her absence.

Through streets bustling with traffic, the coach made its way to the dock. There, the *Lily Belle* was taking on package freight, and Lily couldn't help feeling a bit proud of the ship she now regarded as her own. Its sleek lines, roomy cabins, and stately stack had been designed by Frank Kirby, the most sought-after marine architect in the business.

From a new perspective, she admired the fine image presented by the black hull and pristine white cabins and decks, and she recalled the detailed description Parker had repeated over and over when asked about his vessel. "She's 324 feet long, 77 feet, two inches wide, and weighs 2498 gross tons. She can carry 600 passengers, more on excursions, and has a capacity for 600 tons of freight. Her officers and crew, all 108 of them, are the best on the lakes!"

The *Lily Belle's* raked stack sported a huge white circle in which the designation "S.S. Line" had been lettered in blue. From the stern of the ship, the American flag fluttered proudly, and from her bow flew the white dovetail Sweetwater pennant.

Lily assisted her aunt aboard, settling her in a chair on the upper deck. As the boat began to fill with passengers, their happy chatter mingled with the constant humming of the engines and the occasional thud of a crate landing on the cargo deck in anticipation of the cruise to South Haven.

At the bell signal from Captain Curtiss, the *Lily Belle's* crew began to cast off, and Lily left her deck chair to watch from the railing. The boarding ramp had already been raised from the pier, and when her bow line went slack it was released by a dock worker to be quickly reeled in on board. The procedure was repeated at the stern, and with the shout of "All clear!" the ship moved forward.

Lily couldn't help wondering, as her boat left the

Haynes pier and fell in behind the *Chicago* of the Goodrich Line, whether Alick was watching from his office window, and what he must think each time he saw the *Lily Belle*.

Moving down river, Lily always marveled at the congestion. A car ferry, small passenger boat, and tug followed one another like a family of ducks headed for open water. Smokestacks both on and near the river as far as the eye could see poured forth their tons of black exhaust, enshrouding the metropolis in a gray atmosphere tainted with the odor of commerce.

At the mouth of the river, the dingy waters teemed with all manner of vessels: a barge loaded with coal, a steamer piled high with lumber, a pleasure yacht. Even a sloop bravely vied for her right of way.

Two miles north of the Chicago River, wide sandy beaches, groves of shade trees, and the canals and lagoons of Jackson Park came into view, reminding Lily of the trip she had taken there with her aunt aboard the whaleback excursion steamer, *Christopher Columbus*, from Randolph Street in the heart of downtown, to the World's Columbian Exposition of 1893.

As the shoreline faded from view and the *Lily Belle* headed northeast on the open water, the air grew chill, and Lily took her aunt to the lounge amidships on the deck below. The spacious room featured light oak, and was furnished with round tables to accommodate six and chairs upholstered in thick leather. Tiffany glass lamps provided soft illumination from walls and ceiling, and highlighted a stack casing decorated by a mural of Ulysses. A refreshment stand at the aft end of the lounge offered ice cream sodas and lemonade from its countertop of opal tiling and German silver.

The lounge, designed for the use of both ladies and men,

was divided by pillars on both sides into a series of alcoves which offered cozy conversation nooks with an excellent view of the lake. Lily settled Agatha into one of these, then ordered lemonade for them both. Here, they passed the hour in pleasant conversation until dinner.

At six o'clock, Lily and Agatha joined Hoyt, his chief engineer, and first mate at the captain's table for the evening meal. The dining room, illuminated by Sheffield silver candelabra carried on ivory columns and silver wall brackets, was equipped to seat a hundred, and tonight it was filled to capacity, humming with quiet conversation. A waiter took orders for appetizers, soup, salad, and entree, committing them to memory, and delivering them exactly as requested on gold banded china decorated with the ship's flag and crest.

When Agatha had savored the last mouthful of her raspberry trifle, she lay her napkin aside and addressed her niece. "Despite the management problems you've encountered, my dear, the cuisine and service on the *Lily Belle* are equal to, if not better than that of the Palmer House, in my opinion."

Hearing her aunt's praise, Lily beamed. "Your shrewd judgment coupled with your penchant for avoiding insincere flattery makes the compliment all the more meaningful, Auntie. Now, shall we take fresh air on the promenade deck? It's not exactly the veranda of Mackinac Island's Grand Hotel—"

"But it will do very nicely, indeed," Agatha finished for Lily as they rose to take their leave.

The starboard bow offered a perfect view of the early evening approach to South Haven. The lighthouse marking the south pierhead came into view first, along with a vista of church spires, smokestacks, stately elms, and sandy beaches.

31

With a long blast from the steam whistle, the vessel entered a channel dotted by a sloop, a rowboat, and a pair of gulls. On the rise at the end of Erie Street, Lily's two-storey home peeked through elms and willows, and she regarded her return with mixed emotions.

Within minutes, the *Lily Belle* had passed the catwalk and lime kiln, the tall white Vander Meulen warehouse and the long, squat buildings of Snowhill's lumberyard to nudge the Haynes pier. Here, among the welcoming crowd, a wife toting a toddler son awaited the return of her husband, and the driver of a handsome phaeton parked by the side of the road waiting for his master and mistress to be discharged.

A long whistle blast followed by a short one signaled that the *Lily Belle* had been winched in and secured, and her decks began to clear of passengers. Lily, Agatha, and Margaret hired a coach which carried them along Water Street to Maple, and Erie to the corner of St. Joseph, where stood Lily's Queen Anne home with Eastlake embellishments. Though it would have been considered little better than a guest house in Newport, where Lily had spent other summers, she had grown fond of the place during the two months in which she had overseen the decorating of its interior and planting of its teardrop gardens.

The buggy rounded the circular drive to stop at the front walk, and Lily couldn't help admiring the attractive, wide veranda that surrounded the house on the north, west, and south.

On the carriage seat beside her, Agatha leaned out for a better look at the gray shingled home with green shutters. "Your place is charming, Lily, and so is this town. It's certainly quieter than the city, and thank goodness, cooler. I think I'm going to like it. Take me inside and show me my room. This has been quite a day for an old lady like me, and

32

I'm ready to put my feet up."

"I'll give you the room connecting to mine. You'll have a pretty view of the yard."

Agatha carefully mounted the three front steps, one hand on Lily's arm, her cane in the other, while Margaret followed with the hand luggage.

Inside, the foyer smelled extremely stuffy. "If you don't mind sitting in the front hall for a minute, Auntie, I'll open some windows and let in the fresh air."

"I don't mind a bit, dear. I'll just make myself at home on your settee." While Lily and Margaret threw open the three large parlor windows, and those on the back of the house in the dining room and the library where Parker had made his office, Agatha rested on the burgundy velvet double chair in front of the large fireplace. Beside her was the cherry drop-leaf table she had sent her niece as a gift for the new home. When Lily returned to take her upstairs, Agatha was admiring a photograph of herself and Lily which had been set out among those of family and friends.

"I remember when this was taken. It was two summers ago at Grand Hotel on Mackinac Island." She set it aside and pointed to a small portrait of a bride and groom. "Have you heard anything from the Bartletts lately?"

"Tory's first child is due late this month."

"You don't say!" Agatha got to her feet and with Lily's assistance, began to make her way upstairs. "Such a lovely couple. Maybe we should pay them a visit after the baby is born. We could take the *Lily Belle* to the island for a few days' stay. 'T wouldn't be like the good old days when I took a suite for the summer, but it would be fun, wouldn't it?"

Lily chuckled. "Auntie, your plan sounds lovely. There are only a few things wrong with it. First of all, the *Lily*

Belle doesn't go to Mackinac Island. Secondly, I'll be busy tending to the business of running a steamship line."

"I suppose you're right. You couldn't possibly spare the time," Agatha concluded, her disappointment evident.

Leaning on Lily's arm, she limped her way through the master bedroom at the end of the upstairs hallway, and into the slightly smaller attached room which had been decorated in soft blues, both light and dark. She rested on the satin chaise while Lily switched on the electric wall light and opened the windows. Margaret showed in the coachman who deposited Agatha's trunk carefully on the blue flowered carpet.

Not waiting for Margaret, Lily set about the task of unpacking her aunt's most essential belongings, her thoughts on Agatha's comment about Mackinac. "You know, Auntie, I've been thinking. Perhaps we *should* visit Tory. I'll be too busy from now until the end of the summer, but maybe we could go early in September."

"I'd like that, Lily. I'd like it very much."

When she had finished settling in her aunt, Lily began unpacking in her own room. Though she had wondered how she would feel about returning to the bedroom she had shared with Parker, she realized they had spent so little time in it together, that she had come to regard it much more as her own special place, than as a reminder of her departed husband.

Varnished natural dark woodwork covered walls and ceiling, giving the room almost a shipboard appearance. Three large windows in a bay, and a fourth nearby, all decorated with frilly white curtains, brightened the atmosphere, while the brass double bed, the ponderous Empire chest, and the matching mirrored dresser gave an impression of substance.

Along one wall was a day bed, laden with throw pillows. Above it hung a sketch of the *Lily Belle*, drawn by the renowned maritime artist, Samuel Ward Stanton. In the bay with an excellent view of the port stood a small slant top desk. Lily paused beside it a moment to admire the view of the channel at dusk where the parallel piers reached out from the mouth of the Black River. Both to the north and south of the opening stretched a wide expanse of sand providing a playground for swimmers. Though they were nearly abandoned this time of the evening, Lily could envision swimmers dressed in bathing costumes and frolicking in the breaking waves, as they had been when she had last admired the view on an extremely hot May afternoon.

With a fresh, cool breeze from the lake gently flowing through her room, Lily slept soundly, awakening later than usual the next morning when Margaret tapped on her door at nine o'clock.

"Telegram for you, ma'am."

"Come in, Margaret." Lily boosted herself up on her elbows when the maid entered. "You can leave it on my dresser. I'll be down for breakfast in thirty minutes."

"Yes, ma'am."

When the maid had taken her leave, Lily threw back her sheet and crossed the oval wool rug to the dresser. The telegram had come from Chicago, and she wasted no time opening it. The words she read sent a chill through her.

CHAPTER
4

POSTAL TELEGRAPH-CABLE COMPANY
TELEGRAM

```
Chicago Ill 14 July
A.L.Haynes
          South Haven Mich
Cutting Lily Belle off. As of July 21 no
refueling, docking privileges, ticket
sales at Haynes piers.
          A.Haynes
          8:15 A-
```

"How *could* he?" Lily fumed, slapping the telegram against her palm.

"What's the matter, dear?" Agatha asked sympathetically.

Lily handed her the message and paced across the floor, her bare heels pounding against the parquet patterned oak.

Agatha donned her pince-nez, stared at the missive, then laid it aside. "Never you mind, Lily."

Lily spun around to face her aunt. "Blast him! First, he tries to steal from the *Lily Belle*, and now he acts as if he wants nothing to do with her."

"I suspect quite the opposite is true. He wants everything to do with her."

"What do you mean?"

"He sees she's a profitable venture, and he wants to put you into a tight spot, so you'll sell to him. Never you mind, dear. You'll get along without your agreements with the Haynes Transit Line."

"But he can't do this to me. Parker had agreements with him. I'll hire a lawyer and sue him for breach of contract."

"Lily, are you sure these agreements were written down? I don't remember coming across any such contracts among the papers you brought home from Alick's office."

"Drat him! You're right. Oh, Auntie, I don't have any idea how to arrange for new docking facilities or ticket agents. As for refueling, Parker told me Alick was able to obtain a cheaper rate on coal by contracting to have fuel for all the ships, his and Parker's, delivered to the same place." She threw her hands in the air. "I just don't know where to begin."

"I have a feeling arranging for docking facilities and ticket agents depends more on who you know, and how they feel about you, than anything else. Atlantic shippers have kept Jim Hill out of their waters, and he's about as powerful and rich as they come, where the transportation business is concerned. You've got to get on good terms with the right people to succeed . . . in *any* business." Agatha looked Lily straight in the eye. "I know where I'd begin, if I were you."

Lily shrugged. "Where?"

"With the *Lily Belle's* captain. Aside from Parker, surely he would know the most about operating your ship. And he certainly has a vested interest in her success. Why, just the other day, I read in the paper that many lake captains are out of work because the ships are being built larger now and fewer ship masters are needed. Those who are working are earning only two-thirds the amount they were paid last year. I saw from the payroll expenses we went over the other day that Parker valued your Captain Curtiss somewhat higher than the customary rate. No telling what lengths he'd go to, to secure his position for the remainder of the season."

Lily crossed the room to her window. From there, she could see the *Lily Belle* taking on freight for her run to Milwaukee. "My ship will return to South Haven tomorrow afternoon. We'll be able to meet with Captain Curtiss then. Still, I don't see how Sweetwater Steamship Line can afford the time or money to put up new docks and ticket offices."

"Don't you fret, Lily. I believe in your Captain Curtiss. You had a leasing agreement for the Haynes dock, maybe he can suggest another company willing to do the same. If you find you need more capital, I'd be glad to invest in your company."

"But Auntie, you never invest in anything less solid than the Plymouth rock, and right now, the *Lily Belle* is much more like the *Mayflower*, riding out the waves on a storm-tossed sea until the wind subsides sufficiently for her to safely make port."

"I think I can afford to risk a few thousand dollars in my old age. Wilbur left plenty behind so that even if your ship sank, I'd still have more money than I could spend in this lifetime. Besides, I have faith that when you and Captain Curtiss put your minds together to solve these problems, you'll do fine."

Lily hugged Agatha. "Thanks for the vote of confidence, Auntie." Opening her closet door, she said, "I guess I'd better get ready for breakfast, or Margaret will be terribly unhappy with me for being late. Afterwards, I'll organize the office."

Following breakfast, she carried into the office all the documents pertaining to the Sweetwater Steamship Line and laid them on the pedestal oak table in the center of the room. The table was one of her favorite pieces, done in Empire style with beefy legs.

How she loved this room on the back corner of the first floor. Its three large windows overlooked the extensive side and back yards where fronds of a giant weeping willow swayed in the breeze coming off the lake. To the left of the door stood a four drawer oak filing cabinet, and on top of it, the finest weather instruments money could buy, encased in highly varnished mahogany, were monitoring temperature and barometric pressure.

To the right of the door was a roll top desk Lily had given Parker but which he had rarely used. She slid open the cover. A dozen empty pigeonholes waited filling.

Lily completed her work in the library before luncheon, and following the midday meal, she donned her black bombazine dress and black straw hat, and paid a visit to Dr. Adams's office on Phoenix Street.

Of medium height and build and graying at the temples, the congenial doctor offered a greeting when Lily entered the reception room. Evidently, he had just finished seeing Mr. Pettish, the *Sentinel's* editor and owner. The dark-haired man's expression registered surprise when he saw Lily.

"Good afternoon, Mrs. Haynes. Welcome back," he greeted with forced cordiality. "Are you here to stay, or just in town to settle affairs before returning to your family back East?"

The blatant attempt at news gathering aggravated Lily, but she managed to temper her reply. "I have no plans to return East, Mr. Pettish. Evidently you haven't heard. I'm here to take up my late husband's responsibilities with the Sweetwater Steamship Line."

"So you are," he responded on a note of disbelief. A smirk on his face, he exited the office.

The unpleasant encounter over, Lily faced Dr. Adams and got straight to the point. "I'd like to consult you about certain symptoms I've noticed recently, Doctor."

"Of course, Mrs. Haynes. Come right into my office."

Following a detailed discussion and physical examination, Dr. Adams sat at a desk beneath his diploma from the University of Pennsylvania School of Medicine and studied a calendar.

"I'd say along about the first week in February, you'll be a new mother, Mrs. Haynes."

Though Lily had known of the likelihood, she was not prepared for the reality of Dr. Adams's diagnosis. Until now, she had tried to ignore the changes in her body and avoid thinking about the possibility they represented, but now she must face facts, and the future suddenly seemed much more complicated.

Feeling a bit numb, she paid the doctor and thanked him, and went for a stroll that took her in the direction of the docks.

As she walked down Phoenix toward Water Street, she couldn't help wondering whether she carried a boy or a girl Of one thing she was certain: the prospect of motherhood frightened her. Thank goodness, February was still seven and a half months away. She needed time to adjust to the coming changes.

Before returning home, Lily left a message at the dock-side ticket office for Hoyt to come see her as soon as possible after his return from Milwaukee.

At work in her office once again, she tried to concentrate on the problems Alick had thrown her way, but discovered she could only think of Dr. Adams's news and how her life was about to change once more. She had been sitting at her desk for some time, chin in hand, when she became aware of Agatha beside her.

"Lily, I've been standing here talking to you for at least two minutes, and you haven't heard a word I've said. Are you feeling all right? Perhaps you should see a doctor."

"I'm sorry, Auntie. I didn't mean to ignore you. Come in and sit down." She led her aunt to a chair at the library table and pulled one up beside her. "Auntie, I have something very important to tell you. The fact is, I've just been to the doctor. He says I'm to have Parker's child in February."

Agatha drew a sharp breath. "You don't say." The elderly woman reached for Lily's hand, and brightening, added, "Isn't it time you think of remarrying?"

"Remarrying?" Lily cried.

"I mean no disrespect to Parker's memory, but the task of raising a family is too great for a woman alone. I think that captain of yours would make a wonderful father for your child."

"Auntie, you are impossible!" She emphasized each word. "I dare say the last thing on Captain Curtiss's mind is taking a wife . . . especially a *pregnant* wife."

"Hush, child. Well-bred young ladies don't say such a word out loud."

"And well-bred older women don't go trying to make a match of a widow in my condition with an unsuspecting bachelor."

"Oh, pshaw. I should think he'd be honored to raise the child of his good friend."

Lily's head moved slowly from side to side. "You're forgetting one very important thing, aren't you?"

"What's that, my dear?"

41

"*Love.* Normally, a man and a woman fall in love with one another before they marry."

"Your circumstances aren't normal, Lily. You need a man. You need Hoyt Curtiss. Love comes later."

Lily sighed and returned to her desk. "Auntie, I hope this won't come as a big disappointment to you, but your ways are not mine. I will remarry if and when I find a man I can love enough to live with for the rest of my life, a man who can love me and my child with all his heart."

Though she had turned to the papers on her desk, she did not miss Agatha's quiet statement as she left the room. "My dear, I believe you've already found him."

Lily withdrew into her own thoughts. She had claimed she would marry for love, but she did not like to admit that she had done so the first time, and had been greatly disillusioned.

Parker had loved her, of this she was certain, but he had allowed his love of his dream to take over his life, leaving her in second place to the Sweetwater Steamship Line and the *Lily Belle*.

In Hoyt Curtiss, Lily saw a man who had dedicated his life to his mistress: Lake Michigan. If he had ever had a lady friend, she had probably recognized that she could never compete with the water for his devotion.

Though Lily wished she could disregard her aunt's praise of the captain, she found herself remembering the tenderness and concern he had shown her in the hours following Parker's death, and his continued interest in her well being and the affairs of the Sweetwater Steamship Line. With the remembrance came the realization that Parker had held the utmost respect for Hoyt as his friend and his captain.

Perhaps her aunt had a point about her child needing a

father, but the thought of stepping into another marital relationship only to be deeply disappointed was more than she could bear to contemplate.

Lily was no closer to coming to terms with her dilemma when the following afternoon, she noticed the *Lily Belle* moving up the channel, her decks filled with passengers waiting to be discharged, her colors flying proudly in the offshore breeze. An hour later, Margaret entered the office where Lily and Agatha were analyzing ticket sales.

"Captain Curtiss is here to see you, ma'am."

"Thank you, Margaret. Please show him in."

Lily rose from her chair beside her aunt at the oak table and picked up Alick's telegram. Rereading it one more time, she lay it face down at her place on the table. When Margaret announced Captain Curtiss, Lily couldn't help thinking how dignified he looked in his double-breasted navy blue jacket with the gold braid circling the sleeves.

"Thank you for coming, Captain." When she looked into his kind, brown eyes, she allowed herself for an instant to believe that somehow, this man with the sturdy build would magically solve all her problems. On the heels of that fleeting thought came the realization that only hard work and his genuine concern for her could give her a chance to successfully meet the overwhelming challenges before her.

Lily indicated the empty chair opposite hers at the table. "Please have a seat. I trust your latest crossings went well."

With a stately bearing, he crossed the room, nodding at Agatha on his way. Agatha's wrinkles deepened in a modest smile, and Lily was reminded of how the old woman's pale eyes sparkled whenever Hoyt was around.

He set his cap on an extra chair and sat across from Lily.

43

"We sailed with our cabins and holds full, and a fair breeze across our transom. Couldn't ask for more."

"I'm glad your trip went well," Lily replied, "You'd best savor the experience, because your luck has turned for the worse." She handed him the telegram with a flourish.

Hoyt Curtiss stared silently at the missive for a time, and Lily was beginning to wonder if he had need of reading glasses. Perhaps he was only trying to digest the importance of its contents. She bit her tongue and waited for his reaction.

At last, the captain lay the telegram before him and solemnly regarded Lily. "Th-this is unfortunate news . . . indeed."

"Have you any suggestions how to handle the refueling problem, or obtain new docking and ticketing facilities?"

"I have."

Lily cocked her head in the silent seconds following Hoyt's two sweet words, hoping to encourage him to speak, but by now, she had learned that he would share his plan in his own good time. When he did, he spoke to an attentive audience of two, Agatha taking in every word as carefully as her niece.

"When I was . . . a young man on the lakes . . . I made close friends with a wise . . . older gentleman." He delivered his words slowly, like widely spaced swells against a soft, sandy beach, compared to the choppy waves-against-rocks of Lily's speech. "He served as captain on the *Indiana* and the *City of Milwaukee* . . . and he would've served the *Navarino* if she hadn't burned. He's retired . . . but knows most everyone on Lake Michigan. If you could take Friday's run to Chicago . . . I could introduce you to him. Jack Wilson . . . Mad Jack.

"Mad Jack Wilson, you say?" Agatha perked up. "Why,

44

my late husband knew him. He hauled lumber and bricks for Wilbur after the great fire of '71. 'Twas that fire that destroyed the *Navarino*, if memory serves."

Hoyt nodded. "You remember correctly, Mrs. Atwood."

"Why, you couldn't have been more than a little shaver, yourself, back in '71," Agatha noted. Turning to Lily, she remarked, "And you, my dear, would not grace this world with your presence for another six years."

"Auntie, it isn't polite to speak of a woman's age," Lily gently scolded, though she suspected Agatha was only trying to let Captain Curtiss know she was older than she looked.

"Oh, bosh. I don't mean to embarrass you, my dear. Now what do you say to our taking the boat to Chicago tomorrow?"

"It sounds like our best hope for solving our problems. Captain Curtiss, you can plan on us sailing with you Friday."

"Th-then I'll send word to Captain Jack . . . to expect us. M-my driver will pick you up an hour before departure." He reached for his cap.

Lily retrieved it first, brushing an imaginary piece of lint from the immaculate navy blue twill. "Captain, you needn't rush off. I'll have Margaret serve us lemonade in the parlor, if you can stay." Reluctantly, she handed him his hat.

His mouth turned up ever so slightly. "Thank you . . . I'd like that."

The parlor was the most formal room in Lily's house, with its deep green velvet sofa, pale rose silk draperies, and a light green and pink Aubusson carpet covering most of the polished maple floor. Had she thought more carefully, she would have ordered tea for the front room, instead, where the captain might have felt more relaxed, but she needn't have worried. He seemed as comfortable in her parlor as he had in her Aunt Agatha's in Chicago.

Margaret brought a tray of lemonade and scones, and Lily served her guests, helping herself to two of the biscuits while Agatha told Hoyt of her attraction to South Haven. She hadn't even realized she had taken her third scone, the last on the plate, until Agatha apologized to Hoyt.

"You'll forgive Lily if she seems a bit hungrier than usual. A woman in her delicate condition will naturally experience an increase in appetite."

Though Lily could feel her face color, and wanted to spit fire at her aunt for revealing the news of her coming child, Hoyt's tactful response helped smooth over the awkward moment.

"I hadn't noticed your change in appetite, Mrs. Haynes, but I couldn't miss the happy glow." Hoyt was silently thankful for words that, for once, came without a struggle. "When will your child be born?"

Lily sipped her cooling drink before responding. "In February, according to Dr. Adams, but such news needn't cause you concern, Captain. I'll faithfully uphold my responsibilities to the Sweetwater Steamship Line, and count myself fortunate that the blessed event will occur during the offseason."

Lily couldn't have been more wrong than to think her news wouldn't cause Hoyt concern, though she had tried to reassure him for the wrong reason. Of course, he was concerned about her coming child. Not for the effect it would have on her ability to operate the steamship line, but for the burden it would place on her as a young widow. How he wished he could make these feelings known to her, but the right words would not come, and after moments of trying to spur his tongue to action, he finally gave up the struggle. Checking his pocket watch, he rose, and at last worked his mouth out of its lethargy. "I'd best uphold my responsibilities, also. Until tomorrow morning."

Lily said, "I'll see you out, Captain. My legs have grown tired of sitting." He bid Agatha goodbye, and Lily accompanied him onto the veranda where she paused a moment to inhale the pure lake breeze.

Beside her, Hoyt pulled on his cap, and she couldn't help admiring the way it set off his strong profile. At the corner of his shaded eyes, tiny lines gave his ruddy skin the look of maturity, dependability, and trustworthiness due a man of his experience. His mustache and beard set off a generous mouth with a natural upward curve. Though Hoyt was a man of few words, Lily came to the realization, standing next to him, that he was probably the only man with whom she had spent time in silence, and not felt the compelling need to fill those quiet moments with conversation.

His gaze left the vista of shoreline and pierheads to settle on her, and she imagined that he was thinking how her figure would soon change to include the telling bulge of impending motherhood. Such thoughts returned her to the reason for accompanying him to the veranda, and despite their companionable silence, she felt the urge to make an apology.

"Auntie needn't have told you about my condition. I shall have to have a talk with her. My secret would have kept for another two months, and that's what I would have preferred."

Hoyt appreciated the manner in which Lily's black dress set off the white blond of her hair and the milky tone of her delicate skin. Though the skirt nipped in at the waist, he knew he would find her equally attractive when in several weeks' time, her petite figure had begun to increase.

47

Though she didn't appreciate her aunt's outspokenness about her pregnancy, Hoyt was glad he would not spend another eight weeks unaware. "I won't tell anyone you're in the family way, Mrs. Haynes."

Lily laid her hand on his wrist and offered him a ruffle of a smile. "I know I can count on you to keep mum, Captain. I only wish you hadn't found out in the first place. You've shown such kind regard for my welfare since Parker died. I don't mean to add to your concern."

Hoyt's wide hand covered Lily's small one, and she was unprepared for the current of warmth and tenderness that flowed through her. "Your news . . . brings pleasure, not concern . . . knowing a part of Parker lives on."

"You haven't been feeling guilty over his accident, have you?" Lily suddenly asked. She gave his wrist a tiny squeeze, then withdrew her hand, noting how quickly a sense of isolation flowed in to drown the comfort of his touch. "I would hate to think that was the reason for your calling on me these past two months."

Hoyt shook his head. "No . . . not guilt."

Lily wondered if his visits had resulted, even in the slightest, because he cared about her. As quickly as the question arose in her mind, she silently scolded herself. How utterly improper, she realized, for a widow of only two months to be thinking such a thing. Still, she could not deny Hoyt's attractive qualities, not the least of which were his capacity for compassion and his dependable nature. Nevertheless, he was a Lake Michigan man, and his first priority, in all likelihood, would forever be the water.

Lily changed her focus from the sincerity she read in his expression to the *Lily Belle*, whose pennant could be seen fluttering in the distance. "I imagine you're anxious to return to your duties, Captain, so I shan't detain you any longer. Auntie and I shall be ready when your driver calls tomorrow."

He touched his hand to his brim and stepped off at a lively pace, looking back when he reached the bottom of the drive to wave to the mite of a woman who watched him from the veranda. So many things had been left unsaid, either because he could not physically speak the words, or because Lily's curious circumstances had prevented him.

Though Hoyt could not express his feelings about Lily verbally, neither could he keep from putting them to paper. With the perspective of several hours that had lapsed from the time he first learned she carried Parker's child, he sat at his desk in his quarters aboard the *Lily Belle* and penned his thoughts.

> *July 15, 1897*
>
> *Upon my return from Milwaukee, I received a message of some urgency that Lily Haynes wished to meet with me. The problems foremost on her mind concerned a telegram from Alick Haynes severing agreements for dock leasing, refueling, and ticketing of passengers for the* Lily Belle. *I'm certain Mad Jack can help her make new arrangements.*
>
> *A situation I find even more unsettling came to my attention thanks to the boldness of tongue of Agatha Atwood. That is, Lily Haynes will have Parker's child come February.*
>
> *I am elated, yet overwhelmed with a desire to care for her and her unborn child. I feel a fierce protectiveness inside, and I want to be near her to lend support.*
>
> *I look forward to the birth of Parker's child and*

hope she will let me be a part of its life.

She possesses a strength of spirit and will uncommon in most women today. Each time I am with her, I find myself wanting to be more than the captain of her steamship.

One day, I hope to tell her how fond I have grown of her, but neither of us is ready for such an admission.

Lily pushed back the delicate lace curtain from her bedroom window overlooking the channel and gave silent thanks for a new day that had dawned clear and bright. The sun reflected off the calm lake and glistened off the white wings of a gull that soared close to the surface, fishing for his breakfast. A chorus floated on wings in the morning air, bringing the lyric melody of a robin, the timid chirp of a young sparrow, and the raucous call of a blackbird.

She inhaled deeply of the freshening breeze, pleasantly tinged with the scent of raw wood from the lumberyard two blocks to the north, then turned to the task of readying herself for the trip to Chicago. Feeling calmer than yesterday, and more rested than she had in days, Lily was confident that her excursion would provide the turning point from the difficulties she had been experiencing with Alick Haynes.

Since Lily would be returning to South Haven on the homeward bound run that evening, she packed only a portfolio of ship's paperwork. Hoyt's driver arrived exactly on schedule and soon Lily and Agatha were settled on deck chairs.

The vessel emerged onto the lake, and the Captain headed southwest and increased power. At twenty miles per hour, the *Lily Belle* would make Chicago in a little less than four hours. This trip, Lily decided to take Agatha on a tour of some parts of the ship she had not yet visited.

They passed lifeboats and davits on their way to the Grand Saloon where many of the passengers relaxed in mahogany chairs upholstered in green pan plush and decorated with gold braid. Richly grained mahogany paneled the walls, and covering the ceiling was a mural worthy of display in the finest gallery, depicting a royal reception on board a Spanish galleon of the fifteenth century. The room was well lit by brightly polished bronze torches afixed to pillars in semi-relief which stood between recessed wall panels.

Emerging in the center of the area from the lobby was the grand staircase, its handrail and newel caps of polished brass. Aft of this had been placed small writing tables which were inlaid with wood marquetery and lit by leaded glass lamps. Forward of the staircase stood a huge brass urn holding a giant potted palm, and beyond that, the fruit and periodical stands offering produce pretty enough for a still life, and the most recent issues of *Harper's Bazar*, *Ladies Home Journal*, and *Munsey's Magazine*.

Though they would not be occupying a stateroom on such a brief journey, Lily showed her aunt the satinwood cabin where she and Parker had often stayed, with its built-in curved front dresser, huge shield-shaped mirror, and double brass bed. The brown carpet harmonized nicely with the natural wood, as did the couch, upholstered in two shades of brown pan plush. The bathroom was finished with white enamel walls, and black and white mosaic tile flooring.

From there, Lily and Agatha went to the lounge to pass the time until their arrival.

When the Illinois shoreline was visible, a steward approached Lily, dressed nattily in his white uniform with royal blue braid.

"The captain invites you and Mrs. Atwood to join him in the pilothouse. He thought you might like to see the docking procedures from there."

Lily's face brightened. "Thank you. I would enjoy that very much. Shall we go, Auntie?"

Agatha waved Lily off. "You go on and tell Captain Curtiss thanks, but I'd just as soon sit right here where I won't be in his way."

"I'll return for you once we've tied up," Lily promised.

Escorted by the steward, she made her way forward on the cool, breezy upper deck, past a long line of unoccupied cane-seated, ladder back chairs and several canvas covered lifeboats to the stairs which led to the pilothouse. Surrounded by glass on three sides, the hazy coast was emerging, gradually shedding its grayish, vaporous appearance for a clearer, greener line.

Two enormous ship's wheels dominated the room, and nearby stood the brass chadburn where the captain used a lever to telegraph his orders to the engine room several levels below. The face of the instrument was clearly readable even from a distance: "full," "three-quarters," "slow," and "stand by," while operating ahead, followed by "stop," "finished with engine," and the astern speeds of "slow," "half," "three-quarters," and "full."

Not far from the chadburn, a wall sign posted the code of signals to be used by captain and crew:

```
1 whistle or bell..............Go ahead
1 whistle or bell..............Stop
2 whistles or bells............Back
3 whistles or bells............Check
1 long whistle or 4 bells......Strong
1 long whistle or 4 bells......All right
```
2 whistles or 2 bells, when the engine is working ahead, will always be a signal to *stop and back strong*.

Behind the chadburn and wheels, the navigator's table, fitted with large, shallow drawers, held the most recent Lake Michigan charts. Spread across the table top was one of the southwestern region of the lake, showing exact depths of the coastal waters surrounding the port of Chicago, as well as locations of lights and buoys and the entrance to the Chicago River.

At the ship's wheel farthest forward stood a wheelsman, Hoyt at his side requesting a compass heading. He turned from his task to face Lily, and she couldn't help feeling a bit pleased by the tidy image her captain presented in his visored cap, well fitting jacket, and sharply creased trousers which came to rest atop highly polished black shoes.

His beard was neatly trimmed, and though Charles Dana Gibson had brought the clean-shaven image into popularity during the last two years, Lily was glad Hoyt had chosen not to follow the trend.

Hoyt immediately extended his hand in welcome, his words coming slowly. "I thought . . . you might enjoy watching the approach to . . . Chicago from up here. Have a seat, if you like." He offered her a place on a cane chair, adjusting it to give the best view of the approaching shoreline.

"Thank you, captain, but I'll enjoy the view on my feet. I've done quite enough sitting for the past three hours."

She stayed at the window while Hoyt busied himself with the approach to the harbor.

Entering the river, Lily always wondered at the congestion. A freight steamer, small passenger boat, and tug followed one another like geese behind a pilot boat headed for open water.

Upriver bound, the *Lily Belle* fell in behind the *City of Racine* of the Goodrich Line. The vessels would dock opposite one another at the Rush Street Bridge which was barely visible in the distance.

At the wheel, Hoyt fixed his gaze on the approaching bridge, squinting until his brown eyes had narrowed to slits and his normally smooth forehead was creased with deep grooves. Though he couldn't be certain at this distance and with a parade of vessels before him, the Haynes pier where he had always tied up the *Lily Belle*, appeared to be occupied by a large steamer, leaving him no place to discharge passengers and freight!

CHAPTER
5

Hoyt reached for the chadburn and telegraphed an order to stand by. Momentum would carry the vessel forward until he could make a determination.

"Thad, bring my glasses." Hoyt's unusual request, normally made on the open waters when trying to identify a distant boat, was spoken calmly but firmly, and brought a raising of his navigator's brow. Keeping one hand on the wheel, he put the binoculars to his eyes and waited for a clear line of sight.

His grip tightened on the brass wheel, and his stomach knotted as he gave Thad the glasses. "Tell me what you see."

The navigator, a compact man of thirty with a lock of auburn hair falling over his high forehead, required but a moment to draw his conclusion. "By gum, that's the *Huron Queen* tied up at our pier, and she's taking on passengers and freight!" he burst out. "What the blazes is she doing in *these* waters?"

His words brought Lily from her post at the window. "May I see?" she asked, reaching for the binoculars. Looking through the glasses, she inquired, "Captain Curtiss, am I to conclude we have no place to tie up?"

His gaze left the scene at the dock at the north end of the Rush Street Bridge and took in the more pleasing, but equally troubling vision of Lily, her blond hair peeking out from beneath her black hat. She was so small and dainty, and looked even more vulnerable in her widow's weeds. He remembered the telegram from Alick Haynes and felt tension spread up through his shoulders and down his thighs to his calves when he thought of the injustice the man had done his stepbrother's widow. Though Hoyt tried to answer Lily, his tongue seemed plastered to the roof of his mouth.

Lily lowered the glasses and fixed him with her snappy blue eyes. "Captain, please answer me. Have we no docking facility for our passengers and cargo?"

With an effort, he managed to loosen his tongue. "It appears so, ma'am."

"What are we to do?" Lily fretted.

Hoyt could feel the color rising in his cheeks. "Nothing to be done . . . but drop anchor in the river until . . . the *Queen* has finished loading."

The navigator took a second look through the glasses. "I still don't understand. Why is the *Huron Queen* at Chicago? Where do you suppose she's found all those passengers?"

Hoyt let out a tense breath. "I won't know for certain until I go ashore and . . . talk with Alick Haynes. I would guess he's leased the *Queen* from the Detroit and Cleveland Line and . . . put her in competition with the *Lily Belle*."

"Astounding!" Thad spouted. "Then she's taking on *our* passengers and freight—stealing them right out from under our very bow!"

"Do you suppose it's really true, Captain?" Lily asked, a note of panic in her voice.

His calm words belied the storm that was churning inside him. "I'm afraid so, ma'am."

Anger bloomed forth in bright rosy patches on Lily's cheeks. "But we were supposed to have until the twenty-first of the month to arrange for new docking facilities. Just wait until I see Alick. He'll be sorry. The nerve of the man, blatantly stealing our trade; acting as though he can cut us off just like that." She snapped her fingers. "As soon as I'm ashore, I'm going to give that man a tongue-lashing he'll

56

never forget. He'll be sorry he tampered with Lily Atwood Haynes."

While Lily fumed, Hoyt issued orders to drop one anchor off the bow, and another off the stern. Better to say nothing to a lady while she's in such a state, he figured. Soon enough, like a gale on the lake, she'd blow herself out. Then, maybe she'd be ready to listen to reason. At least, he hoped so.

By the time the crew had finished carrying out Hoyt's orders, Lily had calmed down, at least to the point where she was sputtering rather than spouting. Assigning Thad to keep close tabs on the activity dockside, Hoyt approached Lily, who was intently watching the decks of the *Huron Queen* fill with passengers.

"Ma'am, may I have a word with you in my quarters?"

She turned to face him, a hint of surprise on her face. "Of course, Captain."

He led her down a flight of stairs to his cabin, located beneath the pilothouse, and offered her a chair. She perched on the edge of her seat, her back ramrod straight, hands folded, shoulders erect. Though small, her posture spoke volumes about her feelings.

"Ma'am," he began in his usual slow fashion, "if you don't mind my saying, I . . . I think it would be best if you let me speak to Alick for you."

Her brow rose in a high arch. He could read disagreement in her face and was prepared to strengthen his point with additional arguments, such as not upsetting herself in her delicate condition, but before he could give them voice, her expression softened.

"I understand, Captain. You want a man-to-man talk with him, and I don't blame you. He certainly has made you look the fool, what with our having to anchor out here in the river big as life for everyone to see while the *Huron Queen* slips away with passengers and freight that, in all likelihood, were supposed to be ours. It's only fitting that you have your opportunity to confront him over this humiliating circumstance. If you will be so kind as to give me the address for Captain Wilson, Auntie and I will hire a driver, and wait for you there."

Hoyt nodded and reached for his pen. Though he disliked being reminded of their embarrassing circumstances, he was pleased by her cooperation. He printed the name and address in neat, block letters, giving himself time to organize his next words.

"Thank you, ma'am. I'm sorry for the trouble. I'll be ... along to join you . . . soon as I'm finished with ship's business."

"Sorry? You've no need to apologize to me, Captain Curtiss. After all, it's not your fault about the *Huron Queen*. She certainly presents another twist to the problems Captain Wilson will have to sort out for us." Lily read the address Hoyt handed her. "South Michigan Avenue. Not as fashionable as Lake Shore Drive, but a respectable neighborhood. I'd better go and explain the situation to Auntie. Until later, Captain."

Hoyt discharged his passengers an hour late, and spent another forty-five minutes rounding up enough freight handlers to unload his cargo. It seemed the employees of the Haynes Line had already been paid not to touch anything on the *Lily Belle*.

By the time Hoyt entered the Haynes Transit Line office, he had already confirmed his suspicions about the *Huron Queen*. A large sign had been posted for passengers at the dock, showing the schedule of the *Huron Queen* and giving the exact same route as the *Lily Belle.*

Though Hoyt had found that in life, fair treatment usually brought the same from others, such was not the case with Alick Haynes. More troubling was the way in which he had so quickly turned against Lily, not even keeping his own word that the Sweetwater Steamship Line agreements would be honored for another five days.

Shipping had always been a cutthroat business on the lakes, but this was the first time he had seen it turn so with a woman. Then again, it was the first time he had known of a woman owning a steamship line. Maybe times were changing, and women were found in business positions more often these days, but it was no cause for unfairness in company practices.

With such thoughts in mind, he carried himself a little faster than usual off the dock toward Alick's office, past the receptionist who offered to announce him, up the stairs and through the door, closing it firmly behind him.

Alick looked up from his work. Thank goodness he wasn't with someone. Hoyt had counted on his being alone. From his second-storey window, he had probably been watching the controversy of his own creation that had been playing out at the dock not two hundred feet from his padded, leather-upholstered executive's chair and his walnut desk.

Hoyt placed his hands squarely on the broad desk top and locked his gaze on Haynes's shifting gray eyes. A wily smile crossed Alick's mouth. "I'm busy, Hoyt," he said casually, fidgeting with a paper. "You'll have to come back later."

Had Hoyt been quick of tongue, he could have voiced any one of a million thoughts that came into his head at that moment, but he knew from years of experience that he had best stick to the speech he had been mentally rehearsing for the last two hours.

"Haynes, you want competition, you got it. Let's race. The *Huron Queen* against the *Lily Belle*."

Haynes set aside his paperwork and leaned back, clasping his hands behind his neck, elbows splayed. "A race, eh?" He paused, a picture of studied poise. "What are the stakes?"

"Reputation, and $1,000 to charity in the city of the winner."

He thought a moment before asking, "When would this race take place?"

"One month from today. We'll work out the rules between now and then."

Haynes stood, shook down his pant legs and straightened, extending a hand to the man who stood a good six inches shorter than himself, but broader by far. "One month from today."

Hoyt accepted the bony handshake and concluded that, despite his competitor's superior height, he was far less of a man than anyone he knew.

Haynes walked him to the door. "Of course, we both know the stakes will be much higher, with all the betting on the side by the crew and other interested parties. Should be intriguing, Captain. Let's meet here a week from today to discuss the rules. That will give us both time to think over the situation."

"Neutral territory. The Palmer House."

Though Haynes appeared less than enthusiastic, he nodded agreement. "The Palmer House, it is. Until then, Captain."

*   *   *

The coach came to a halt in front of an attractive three-storey brownstone town house on South Michigan Avenue, and Lily found herself admiring the decorative wrought iron fence that surrounded the home, and the more intricate iron railing leading up the dozen or so steps to the front entrance. Above the double door, a charming balcony extended from a second floor bedroom.

She paid the driver, tipping him well, and asked him to wait until she and Agatha were inside before pulling away. Chicago was warm and humid this sunny July day, far more uncomfortable than the temperature at South Haven or on the lake, and she did not want her elderly aunt to be stranded in the heat without transportation if the meeting with Captain Wilson did not come off as planned.

Moments after ringing the bell, a servant opened the door, and Lily was thankful to put such worries aside and wave the driver off.

The butler, whose obsequious manner and British accent bespoke service in some London household, led Lily and Agatha into the library, a long, hardwood-panelled room devoid of feminine frills, but embellished with mementos of a lake faring man. A piece of varnished driftwood, which had been carved in bas relief to resemble a steamer, decorated the mantelpiece dominating the long left wall. In a place of honor above the mantle hung a painting of the *Walk-in-the-Water*, the third steamer to ply the Great Lakes and the one generally considered to have ushered in the age of steam on the inland waters. It was signed by Captain Wilson himself.

Before the red brick fireplace, a sprawling brown leather armchair and matching foot rest, positioned to take best advantage of heat from a fire, occupied the center of the only rug in the room, a four foot-by-six foot burgundy and tan oriental carpet.

More seating was available at the table near the built-in bookcase at the back of the room. Here, Lily and Agatha settled themselves on Louis XIV reproduction chairs that had been sufficiently padded beneath bargello upholstery to afford a long reading in comfort.

While waiting for Captain Wilson to join them, Lily laid out the papers she had brought on the library table, then browsed the bookcase to take a measure of the man she was about to meet. His taste, she discovered, ran to the classics bound in rich leather covers, while in the empty spaces between, a polished brass compass and equally shiny ship's bell, retrieved from the *Navarino*, spoke volumes of his nautical past.

When Captain Wilson entered the room, Lily quickly observed the resemblance to Hoyt's broad physique. With gray hair and full beard and mustache to match, however, Wilson was easily thirty-five years Captain Curtiss's senior. Still, his wide shoulders and trim waist could have belonged to a much younger man, Lily concluded. He limped toward Agatha with the aid of a walking stick

"Mrs. Atwood, it's been ten years or more since we last met." He greeted her in a gravelly voice. "I must say, you look as though it hasn't been more than five." He kissed Agatha's hand.

"Now, Mad Jack, you needn't flatter an old woman," Agatha chided, though her sparkling eyes and wide smile belied her words.

Turning to Lily, he added, "And this attractive young woman must be your niece. Well, well, I am indeed a fortunate man to be called upon by such a charming pair of ladies."

"Pleased to meet you, Captain Wilson. I apologize for

Captain Curtiss's absence. He has been unexpectedly detained at the dock, but I'm certain he'll be along soon."

"No point in starting without him. Why don't I have Ridgley serve us refreshments, and we can reminisce about the old days until Hoyt comes."

Lily could have been mistaken, but from the look of pleasure on Captain Wilson's face, he seemed glad to have their company to himself for a while.

As they sipped root beer, Agatha and the captain recalled former times in the city.

"Seems like an age since the fire of '71," the captain remarked.

"Think of it. Over three hundred city blocks in ashes," Agatha remembered.

"And the *Navarino*, as well. How I had looked forward to serving as her master."

"Instead, you and Wilbur made names for yourselves in construction, building the new Palmer House and such."

The captain gave a nostalgic nod. "Yes, we did all right for ourselves . . . until Wilbur got tangled up by mistake in the Haymarket Square riot in '86."

"He was lucky to come out of the bomb blast alive." Agatha thought back to the endless days and nights, slowly nursing her husband to health. "By the time he was back on his feet, we'd gained a new meaning for life," she recollected.

She was obviously enjoying this chance for reminiscing, and Captain Wilson was a skilled conversationalist. The two seemed so delighted with each other's company, Lily was glad Hoyt had been delayed.

Agatha and the captain were comparing their opinions of the World's Columbian Exposition when Hoyt entered the library, quickly tucking away the handkerchief with which he had been mopping his brow.

"Welcome, son. Glad you're here." Captain Wilson pulled out the empty chair beside him. "Can't say I'm sorry you were late. Your lady friends have been keeping me good company. Don't think I've enjoyed myself this much since the day I put my money on the *Columbus*, and she beat the *Virginia* into Milwaukee by a good three-quarters of a mile. Now, you know I'm not a betting man, but that day, I made myself—"

"An extra fifty dollars," Hoyt finished with him. They both chuckled, but Hoyt's levity vanished quickly, a solemn mask sliding into place.

Ridgley returned with a glass of root beer for Hoyt, and Wilson dismissed the butler with a request to close the library doors before getting down to business.

"Now tell me, son, what was this trouble you were having at the dock today? Has Alick Haynes come up with some new torment to add misery to your life?"

Hoyt finished half the contents of his glass seemingly in one swallow before attempting to answer. "Haynes...Haynes is running the *Huron Queen* on the same routes as the *Lily Belle*. He set up a schedule to...purposely interfere with ours at the dock."

Wilson's head moved slowly from side to side. "I'd have thought he'd wait until the twenty-first to try something like this. Whatever happened to the days of honor among men on Lake Michigan? I suppose they're gone forever."

Hoyt raised a finger. "They're not gone yet. I...I challenged the *Huron Queen* to a race one ... month from now. We—"

"You what?" Lily cut in.

Agatha broke into a broad grin. "Bless your soul, Captain Curtiss. A race. Just think of it, Lily. The *Belle's* captain against the *Queen's*. What a wonderful stroke of genius! Now, Captain Curtiss, you can prove once and for all just whose passenger ship will rule Lake Michigan. By golly, I hope you send the *Huron Queen* back to her own waters in disgrace."

"I'll try my best, ma'am."

Captain Wilson tapped his index finger against the table top. "This will require a strategy session, Hoyt. Where will the race be run?"

"The rules will be decided . . . at a meeting a week from today."

"Ah, good. That gives us time to think. First, we'd better deal with the problems closer at hand. I've come up with some possibilities for dock leasing and refueling." He reached behind him to pull a folder from a built-in drawer beneath the bookcase.

Lily opened her portfolio and laid the *Lily Belle's* schedule before him. "Since we're now in competition with another vessel on the same route, perhaps you could come up with some ideas here, too."

Captain Wilson nodded. "I like the way you think, Mrs. Haynes. That very possibility was just going through my mind, and I believe I have some thoughts for you to consider."

Lily soon discovered that despite Captain Wilson's weak legs, he had made great strides toward solving her problems. The Hurson Line of Chicago would lease her prime dock space and handle tickets for her passengers at a reasonable fee. As for refueling, the Crescent Coal and Mining Company on Dearborn Street would be able to supply excellent quality steam coal at the right price, and would guarantee delivery on schedule every time.

Dock leasing in Milwaukee would be available through a lumber yard owner Wilson had hauled for, but South Haven presented a more difficult problem. "A new dock in your home port might require a little more time and money," he concluded.

Her eyes twinkling, Agatha laid her hand on his wrist. "Say, Mad Jack, want to buy a few shares in a promising new steamship company? It has an excellent captain, and the most experienced consultant in all of Lake Michigan shipping."

Wilson leaned back and let out a deep-throated, jovial laugh. His loud chortle soon had Agatha and Lily giggling, and within moments, even Hoyt had begun to chuckle so that the whole room rang with laughter.

From the corner of her eye, Lily noticed that the library door had opened a crack. Evidently the hilarity had raised Ridgley's curiosity, and he had decided to peek in.

When the last chuckle had died down and Lily was drying her teary eyes, she realized a year or more had passed since she had laughed so hard. Certainly she had not found anything so entertaining during her months of marriage to Parker, who had been serious to a fault.

In control of himself again, Wilson responded, "With such prospects as the Sweetwater Steamship Line's, Mrs. Atwood, how can I refuse to invest?"

She rapped the table with her fist. "Good. Lily, we've just solved the dock problem at South Haven. I'm sure a man as prosperous as Captain Jack could see his way clear to funding the leasing of a pier and ticket office there."

"You are a sly one, Mrs. Atwood," he accused, though the grin on his face said he was clearly enjoying the ruse.

"Now that you've decided to financially back the Sweetwater Line," Lily said, "maybe you could give us

66

FREE DELUXE BIGWATER NOTE CARDS

To get four free ivory note cards depicting the scene found on page six of *The Captain and the Widow*, and matching envelopes, send:

➤ Your original filled-out reader survey from the back of *The Captain and the Widow* (no photocopies)

➤ Your sales receipt with purchase price of *The Captain and the Widow* circled showing name and address of the store where you bought the book

➤ This certificate filled out with your name and address

To: Bigwater Note Cards, P.O. Box 177, Caledonia, MI 49316

Name _____

Address _____

City/State/Zip _____

some suggestions for beating our competition."

"The *Lily Belle's* success will depend a great deal on the expertise of her captain and his chief engineer, but as the owner of the line, Mrs. Haynes, here are some suggestions you might consider.

"First off, I'd adjust the schedule so that your competition is not departing earlier than you are from any given port. Also, change your rates. Offer lower fares."

"Lower fares?" Lily questioned, slightly aghast.

Captain Jack raised a staying hand. "It's just a suggestion. It would give you a definite edge. Of course, it could also lead to a price war.

"A third option is purchasing higher quality coal. If your captain and engineer are willing to push your engines to the limit, you can come in ahead of the competition, and everybody wants to be cruising with the winner. Success here could increase your load each trip."

"You've given me a lot to think about, Captain Wilson. I appreciate all the trouble you've gone to. Next week, I'll issue a new schedule, and I'm going to order a better quality fuel, too. I'll have to give our fares some consideration." She consulted her watch, then gathered up her notes. "I see it's time to get Captain Curtiss back to the docks. Thank you so much, Captain Wilson. if ever you want passage on the *Lily Belle*, please be my guest." She handed him a season pass good for complimentary tickets on any run.

His hazel eyes sparkled as he read the card. "Why, thank you."

Agatha warned, "See that you make use of it. I expect you to show up in South Haven one of these days and pay us a call."

"I intend to do just that, Mrs. Atwood. And, Hoyt, stop by next time you're in port and we'll discuss the race."

"I'll see you on Tuesday," Hoyt promised.

The cab wound its way through thick afternoon traffic, arriving at the dock an hour before the five o'clock departure of the *Lily Belle*. Lily feared her ship's decks would be rather barren of passengers this trip, and unfortunately, the expectation proved true. At five o'clock, she counted only two dozen faces on a vessel which normally carried hundreds.

Dinner was served at six o'clock, and the dining room seemed sadly empty, with only four of its seventeen tables occupied.

After the waiter had taken their orders, Lily turned to Hoyt. "Captain, I'm almost afraid to ask. Have we any freight aboard, this trip?"

His head moved slowly from side to side. "Precious little, Mrs. Haynes."

"I suppose we won't even cover the cost of our fuel this time, let alone the expenses of the crew."

"Now, Lily, don't you go fretting over circumstances that couldn't be helped," Agatha chided. "You've got Captain Jack and me investing in your boat's future, and you've employed the best ship's master on the lakes in Captain Curtiss." She winked at Hoyt.

Hoyt raised a finger, preparing to make a statement. "Next week, trade will improve."

"Is that a promise, Captain?" Lily inquired.

"You bet."

Conditions on the deck following dinner were cool and breezy, with a flaming ball of orange lowering toward the horizon off the port rail. Though the promenade deck seemed ominously empty, evidently too chilly for the other passengers, Lily enjoyed the peaceful swooshing of water being carried over the sidewheel, the clean scent of the bracing lake air, and its soft rush against her cheeks.

She had left Agatha sitting in the lounge, rereading one of her volumes of Benjamin Franklin's quotations. With her admonishment to "enjoy the present hour," and her assurance that she would be perfectly content until the ship docked in South Haven, Lily had felt confident to go off by herself for a while. Agatha seemed to know her niece could use time alone to reflect on the recent development.

Lily was wondering how her ship would fare against the competition when she noticed Hoyt approaching.

As he neared the widow, his thoughts tumbled, one over another, in a strange succession he could never have voiced. Curiously, he felt much about her as he did his ship—protective, wanting to harbor her from all storms, and respectful in his awareness of her strengths and frailties.

He was drawn to Lily in a way he found difficult to explain, even to himself. As a Lake Michigan man, he had taken note of the sleek lines and fine finish of many a ship, but his attraction to Lily could hardly be described in similar terms.

True, he felt sorry for her, facing a plethora of difficulties with the Sweetwater Steamship Line that would have set many an experienced business investor to shaking in his shoes. But his feelings surpassed those of plain old sympathy.

He couldn't help appreciating the lovely vision she made now, with strands of her fair hair blowing free of her black hat, cheeks pink from the cool breeze. Of course, the most important measure of a lady was not her outward appearance, but was contained within.

Obviously, Agatha Atwood meant a great deal to her niece, and unlike many young people who were only concerned with attaining, or in Lily's case, maintaining wealth and social status, Lily showed a genuine concern for her elderly aunt.

Hoyt stood beside the young woman, resting his elbows on the rail and looking out across the water. Accustomed to her chattering ways, he assumed that only a matter of seconds would pass before Lily initiated conversation. He was not disappointed.

"Well, Captain, just between us, how do you feel about serving as master of the *Lily Belle*, now that we're into this mess with the *Huron Queen?*"

He leaned back, half facing her. "My feelings about the *Lily Belle* . . . haven't changed. She's the finest ship I've ever served . . . and I wouldn't change places with anyone."

"Not even the captain of the *Queen?*"

A wry smile appeared on his lips. "*Especially* not the captain of the *Queen*." Hoyt was pleased with the prompt manner in which he had replied, escaping quickly for once from the barrier reef that usually held his tongue in check.

"I'm glad to know you're not entertaining thoughts of abandoning ship yet, Captain Curtiss," Lily teased.

Hoyt, suddenly sober, looked straight into Lily's bright blue eyes, a shade that put even the clear waters of Lake Michigan to shame, and quietly stated, "I could never do that, Mrs. Haynes. You can count on me. Always."

The seriousness of his declaration seemed to chase away Lily's lightheartedness. Her response was subdued and thoughtful. "Always is a long time, Captain Curtiss. Always is . . . " she struggled to keep her voice from cracking, "like in a wedding vow . . . "

70

CHAPTER
6

Lily turned away, and Hoyt knew she was hiding her silent tears from him. Praying she would not be offended by his boldness, he made her face him again. "I have a big shoulder, Mrs. Haynes."

Lily struggled to keep her crying in check, but the touch of Hoyt's strong, gentle hands reminded her of how much she missed the simple affections of a man. Though she'd had no intention of doing so, she rested her head against Hoyt's shoulder and let the tears fall.

Hoyt put his arm loosely about Lily and hoped that if anyone were watching, the innocent display would not become fodder for nasty gossip. The fragile scent of roses teased his nostrils, and the delicate woman in his embrace gave rise to a protectiveness within him.

He realized he had not held a lady in his arms since he had danced at Parker and Lily's wedding seven months ago. He remembered, too, thinking then that his friend was making a mistake, taking for his bride this spoiled debutante from the East. Now, he wondered if perhaps it was Lily who had made the mistake, ending up a widow before her time. How he wished he could have spared her this heartache.

Giving herself over to Hoyt's comforting, Lily leaned against his strong support, burying her face in her handkerchief. Though she tried to stifle her whimpering, it grew louder, and all that was going wrong in her life demanded release. "Oh, Captain . . . my life is in such a mess," she blubbered.

"There, now." Hoyt patted her arm. "It's not so bad."

"Oh, but it is!" She gulped for air. "The ship is running empty... Parker went and died on me... and now I'm going to have his baby!" Lily gave herself up to choking sobs that wracked her body.

In his arms, Lily bawled all the louder, and he held her tighter. "Please calm down... Mrs. Haynes. I'll help you all I can."

His soothing reassurance seemed to have a calming effect on Lily. Her crying gradually stopped. She released herself from his embrace and turned away.

How foolish and ashamed Lily felt. Her emotions seemed to be controlling her these days. She blew her nose and dried her eyes, and with one last sniff, faced Hoyt again. "I'm sorry, Captain Curtiss. I had no right to burden you with my personal problems."

"I don't mind, Mrs.—"

"And would you please stop calling me Mrs. Haynes?" she interrupted, obviously annoyed. Sweetly, she added, "I mean, I'd prefer Lily when we're not on company business, Captain Curtiss."

"And I'd prefer Hoyt."

"That's fair, Hoyt." She consulted the watch pinned to her lapel. "I'll have to check on Auntie soon or she'll worry that I've fallen overboard. Before I go, I wanted to ask whether you meant what you said at dinner about the race. Do you honestly think we have a good chance of beating the *Huron Queen*?"

All spontaneity gone, he silently worked his jaw before answering. "Victory won't come easy... but I intend to claim it. I'm confident enough in this ship ... to stake my future on her."

"*And* your own expertise. You've got mettle, Hoyt. I hope the *Lily Belle* performs to your expectations."

"She will."

The following morning, Lily wrote an announcement giving a new schedule and rates for the *Lily Belle*, and placed it in the Sunday edition of the newspapers serving her three ports of call. Though she incurred additional costs to send telegrams to Chicago and Milwaukee, she considered the expense worthwhile.

She visited Mr. Snowhill, who owned the lumberyard west of the Haynes Steamship Line pier and ticket office, and made arrangements for a new facility that placed her ship a hundred yards closer to the channel. As Captain Wilson had promised, she paid dearly for the leasing privilege and construction of her own ticket office, but such were necessities in her home port.

She put a call through to Mr. C.W. Gilmore of the Crescent Coal and Mining Company and requested the best steam coal he could produce, then she typed a notice to her pursers and stewards authorizing them to accept the pass she had issued to Captain Jack Wilson.

Lily was dockside when the *Huron Queen* and *Lily Belle* loaded passengers for Chicago on Tuesday morning, and from what she could tell, they both sailed half full. She was pleased to see Hoyt pull ahead once he had cleared the channel, but dismayed when the *Queen* steamed into port a full five minutes ahead of the *Lily Belle* later in the evening.

The situation repeated itself on Wednesday, when the two steamers sailed to Milwaukee. On Friday, Lily went to Chicago to accompany Hoyt to the meeting with Alick which was to take place at the Palmer House concerning rules for the race. Though she had asked Agatha to join her, the older woman had declined, saying the business of racing could be best decided by those most directly involved.

73

When Hoyt and Lily arrived at the hotel, they were shown into a room furnished with a long mahogany table, gold wallpaper flocked with burgundy fleur-de-lis, and chairs thickly padded and upholstered in burgundy leather.

Alick was already seated at one side of the table, along with the strapping, rough-cut engineer of the *Huron Queen* whom he introduced to Lily as Max Taggart.

Hoyt seemed to know Max and greeted him respectfully, then held a chair for Lily and seated himself across from Alick. "I expected your captain to be here," he said.

A sly smile overtook Alick's narrow mouth. "You're looking at him. I'll be serving as master the day of the race, Curtiss. It's me against you."

Though in times past, Alick had served as master on some of his railroad car ferries, Hoyt knew he had been dockside as superintendent in recent years, and sensed his own advantage, being familiar with the lake waters which changed yearly. He also had the benefit of advice from his meeting Tuesday with Mad Jack, a veteran who knew all the tricks in the book on how to get the most from a steamer.

"Suits me, Haynes," Hoyt said coolly. "Let's establish time and place."

A discussion ensued as to the advantage of racing over a route currently covered by the steamers, or one on neutral waters. After several minutes, the start and finish points were set.

A date for the race was chosen more quickly, both Hoyt and Alick agreeing that two weeks would allow sufficient time for preparation.

Further rules, describing in detail the terms of the race, were laid out until Lily had several pages of notes which she read back to the captains and reworded until each gave his signature of approval.

Lily was glad when the meeting ended, and she could return to the *Lily Belle*. She was even more gratified to discover that Jack Wilson was waiting in the pilothouse, aboard for the trip to South Haven.

"Captain Jack, it's nice to see you again," Lily greeted him. He occupied a chair by the window, and started to get up when he saw her. "Ah, ah. Stay where you are," she scolded, coming quickly to him with hand outstretched.

Wilson took her hand in both of his, a smile spreading over his face. "My, my. Aren't you a sight for these tired eyes. I do believe you've gotten even prettier since last I saw you." He winked at Lily as Hoyt came up behind her.

She laughed lightly. "Flattery will get you everywhere —at least everywhere the *Lily Belle* sails," she responded. "You're staying with Auntie and me, I assume."

Before he could answer, Hoyt shook a warning finger at his friend.

"Mrs. Haynes, you know I'd love to stay at your place," Captain Wilson began, "but—"

Lily put on a frown. "But what?" Offering Hoyt a reproving look, she turned again to the old gentleman. "Has Captain Curtiss made you a better offer?"

"I wouldn't exactly say *better*. I'm sure your accommodations could beat his couch any night of the week. But with the race coming up, I did promise I'd talk strategy with Hoyt and Engineer Bates once the rules were set. How did the meeting go?"

While Hoyt saw to the preparations for casting off, Lily read the rules to Captain Wilson. Later, over a dinner launched with caviar appetizers and cold strawberry soup, followed by salad greens with hot bacon dressing and broiled whitefish, and topped off with chocolate mousse, Captain Wilson shared suggestions for making the most of the opportunity the race offered to improve traffic on the *Lily Belle*.

Throughout the meal, the excellent view from the dining room had allowed them to keep tabs on their position compared to the *Huron Queen*. By the time they had finished their coffee, as had happened on past return trips, the *Queen* had pulled ahead.

The two captains returned to the pilothouse and the business of trying to outrun the *Queen*, while Lily adjourned to the lounge to copy in a more legible hand her notes from the meeting. She would submit them to the editors of both the South Haven and Chicago newspapers, thereby giving official notice of the upcoming race.

Though the *Queen* again outran the *Lily Belle* on the homeward stretch, the gap had narrowed considerably from earlier trips to a mere ship's length before the steamers made their turn into the dusk-shrouded channel.

Lily watched from the starboard rail of the upper deck as the *Lily Belle* was made secure at the dock. She was surprised to spot Agatha on Water Street below, sitting in a hired coach alight with gas lanterns. She hadn't expected her aunt to meet her, and was about to descend the stairs to the lower deck when Hoyt's hand on her shoulder stopped her.

"May . . . may I see you home?" He nearly bit his slow tongue in frustration over his stammer, but managed to unsnag it with his explanation. "Agatha is here for Jack. He wired her before he left Chicago . . . and asked to take her for a drive . . . this evening. He was too embarrassed to tell you himself."

Lily offered Hoyt a puzzled look. "Then he *is* staying with us tonight."

Hoyt shook his head. "He's not ready for that yet.

Getting him here for a drive with Agatha . . . was difficult enough."

An impish smile curved Lily's mouth. "You're quite a matchmaker, Captain Curtiss. Of course you may see me home. I wouldn't interfere with a budding romance for anything in the world."

Hoyt offered to hire a rig, but the evening air was so pleasant, Lily insisted on walking the three short blocks to her home on the hill. By the time they arrived on Lily's veranda, darkness had nearly overtaken the port, and white dots of light marked the homes below.

A twinge of nerves momentarily forced Hoyt's tongue against the roof of his mouth as he thought of the surprise he had planned for Lily this evening, but eagerness to know her reaction freed it long enough to say his piece. "Lily—" He looked into her angelic face. "When you go inside, please visit your aunt's room, then come back and tell me what you think."

"What on earth are you talking about?"

Hoyt shook his head in response, and turning her about, opened the front door and gently nudged her across the threshold.

His heartbeat quickened while he waited, but a nervous smile added curl to his mustache as he anticipated Lily's return.

Lifting her skirt higher than usual, Lily took the stairs in a very unladylike two-at-a-time fashion. She tried to imagine what could possibly have changed in her aunt's room since she had left home that morning for Chicago. Perhaps Agatha, with her penchant for all shades of violet, had wished to replace the blue decor with colors more to her liking but had been reluctant to voice her preference for fear of hurting Lily's feelings. Lily had, after all, spent a full two months decorating the house, fitting out the rooms with the utmost care so they would blend into a harmonious symphony.

Lily's first indication of changes in the upstairs came before she even reached Agatha's room, which was accessible only from her own. Laid out on Lily's bed were several articles of curious origin: cotton night dresses, flannel skirts, a flannel dressing gown, a dozen face towels, a pair of bedroom slippers, two pairs of open drawers, and a large apron. She puzzled over the last, then taking it into account with the other items, realized these supplies were intended for her time of delivery—the apron being for the doctor.

Burning with curiosity as to what awaited her in Agatha's room, she laid aside the huge apron and hurried through her aunt's door, turning the light switch on her way in. Oddly, none of her aunt's belongings could be found in the room.

Though the blue flowered carpet and coordinating striped wallpaper remained exactly as before, nearly all the furnishings had been removed and replaced. Where Agatha's bed had once stood, was now a magnificent baby cot in gold leaf finished brass, its basket entirely edged with full lace ruffles. Suspended from its hood was a generous drape of white silk and lace which could be drawn about the entire bed—fabric so gorgeous it took Lily's breath away. She hurried to take a closer look, running her fingers over the delicate material. The bed itself was lined with a little mattress that had been covered with the finest white satin.

Lily's heart came to her throat, so touched was she by Hoyt's thoughtful gesture. She wondered how she could thank him when she realized the baby bed was not the only new piece of furniture in the room.

Beside the window stood a reed rocker, its ornamental

78

back curved into the shape of a heart. Lily had never seen a prettier chair, and trying it out, she found it fit her perfectly.

She had rocked but a moment when she noticed that against the opposite wall was a spanking white changing table complete with baby powder and powder puff, a box of cold cream, a fine sponge, a paper of large safety pins and another of small, a pair of round-tipped scissors, and of course, two dozen diapers. Lily lifted the cover off the baby powder, dabbed a puff onto the back of her hand, and inhaled the innocent scent, thinking in seven short months such essence would become a part of her daily life.

She held one of the soft cotton diapers against her cheek, then laid it out and folded it as if for a girl. Taking another, she folded it as if for a boy, then removed large pins from their paper and pinned them in place, wondering which style would be appropriate for her first child. No matter, her newborn would no doubt be the object of Hoyt's affection and generosity, which had already flowed so abundantly she could not keep a tear from spilling down her cheek.

Her single tear threatened to form a stream when she noticed that beside the changing table stood a tiny chest painted bright white, its drawers partway open to reveal several more necessary items for her newborn infant: eight belly bands of infants' flannel, four flannel barrie coats with muslin bodies left open like an apron, four wool undershirts so small she could not help marveling at their tiny size, six muslin night slips, two flannel skirts, four pairs of knit socks, and two blankets of fine merino bound with ribbon—one of pink; the other, blue.

In the bottom drawer, Lily found perhaps the prettiest of all the infant necessities—a white cashmere wrapper embroidered with pink and blue floss at the collar, cuffs, and around the edges, the stitches fine enough for an emperor's

79

heir. She hugged the precious garment to her, thinking how drastically its pure innocence contrasted with her somber black dress. Was her mourning symbolic of the difficulties that had plagued her past, and the infant's togs a presage that tomorrow whispers joy?

Lily had not pondered the thought long enough to come to any conclusion when she realized the closet door had been left ajar, and more tiny clothing was hanging inside. Returning the wrapper to its drawer, she opened the closet wide to admire two white frocks. The first had a front opening, a collar of hand lace and more of the same at the wrists, and tiny little blue bows at the throat, partway down the front, and on the shoulders and cuffs.

The second small children's garment buttoned down the back and featured a yoke trimmed with a double flounce of wide lace, more of the same at the shoulders, and a border of pink stitching near the hem. Lily couldn't help smiling when she envisioned her child toddling about in such pretty, frilly attire.

As she rehung the dress on the closet rod, she suddenly remembered Hoyt was waiting on the veranda for her reaction, and at the same instant, she noted the open attic door with a note tacked to it.

"See upstairs," was hand printed in bold upper case letters, and beneath it in her aunt's unsteady hand, was an addendum. "Everything in nursery and playroom is from your captain."

Lily removed the note and decided she would not venture to the third floor, one huge plastered room that covered the entire level. Not yet, anyway. She rang for Margaret.

The maid arrived in the nursery too quickly to have come from her servant's quarters, and Lily was certain she must have been in the hallway all along.

Struggling to hide the smile lurking at the corners of her mouth, Margaret answered, "Yes, ma'am?"

"Margaret, where, may I ask, are Aunt Agatha's belongings?" Lily's inflection rose at the end in mock accusation.

"They've been moved to the southeast bedroom at her request, ma'am," came the all too confident reply.

Attempting to maintain a pretense of normality, Lily responded, "Very well. Captain Curtiss is on the veranda. Will you please show him into the nursery?"

"Yes, ma'am."

Hoyt paced the wooden porch, wondering what was keeping Lily so long upstairs. Could she have forgotten he had asked her to come down and tell him what she thought? No, he reasoned. She was far too polite to allow any kindness to go unacknowledged, even if unappreciated.

Suppose she didn't approve of the changes he had schemed to put into place, with the help of Agatha and Margaret? Maybe he had misjudged Lily and his idea of showering her with gifts for the coming child was all a big mistake.

No, Agatha had thought well of the plan. Surely he could trust her judgment.

His feelings, as if riding a pendulum, swung again from confidence to apprehension when Margaret asked him to follow her up the stairs to the nursery, where she left him, unannounced.

Lily was standing beside the baby cot when he arrived in the doorway, evidently unaware of his presence. He saw her in profile, head bent as if looking in on a sleeping child, and imagined how she might appear in the first weeks of new motherhood, her mourning black traded for a white dressing gown, worries over business having been replaced by the

81

simple pleasures of her newborn child.

She looked up, her intense blue eyes hazy with emotion, and invited him in with the slightest gesture.

Lily was becoming quite flustered over her quick mood changes. One moment, she was happy, the next, so sentimental she could barely keep from crying, and in the short time since Margaret had gone to fetch Hoyt, she had managed to switch from lighthearted to maudlin. Seeing concern in Hoyt's expression—the doubtful look in his compassionate brown eyes, the tiny droop at the corners of his mustache, the way he worked his jaw when apprehension had set in—made her want to go to him this instant, hug him about the neck, and tell him how absolutely overwhelmed she was with his kindness and caring.

But such a response would be inappropriate. Words would have to suffice. The trouble was, the loquacious Lily who could normally talk circles around any three people, now encountered difficulty saying the two words which would serve most appropriately on an occasion such as this.

Clearing her throat in an attempt to keep her voice from cracking with emotion, she managed a barely audible, "How can I ever thank you?"

Hoyt shrugged. He couldn't move, as though he'd run his keel on a sand bar. Then Lily smiled and a freeing tide seemed to rush in. She was holding the note about the playroom in her hand.

"I haven't been upstairs yet, Hoyt," Lily explained rather weakly. Trying for more conviction, she added, "And furthermore, I'm not going unless you come with me."

He was pleased her feistiness had begun to resurface. Her spirited declaration fortified him, as a sail with a fresh breeze, and he had no trouble taking her by the elbow and starting up the stairs. Even his tongue seemed dislodged at last. "Your aunt and Margaret deserve the thanks," he said.

"Forgive my saying so, but that's just like you, Hoyt Curtiss. I can appreciate their part in your conspiracy to fit me out for motherhood, but your own kindness far exceeds my imaginings, and I haven't even reached the playroom yet."

"Then you'd better learn to think bigger . . . where I'm concerned," said Hoyt, helping her up the last half-flight.

When Lily stepped into the playroom, her eyes grew so large she thought they just might pop out of their sockets. The floor had been divided into two areas. One end had been furnished for a girl, the other for a boy.

"This is too much, Hoyt. Just too much," Lily said with awe, yet she couldn't resist perusing the girl's end.

The area had been arranged like a playhouse with dividers creating little rooms. In the wash room was a toy washing machine, with its scrub board, wringer, and bucket all painted in bright colors. Beside it stood a clothes reel and pins.

The next room had been furnished with a folding table and a tin kitchen set, including pots and pans large enough for small loaves or cakes. Lily could imagine her daughter, in a few years' time, asking Margaret to bake some of her batter in these tiny little containers.

Nearby, in the dining area, a miniature sideboard displayed a silver finish Brittania tea set handsomely decorated in bas-relief. The fancy filigree sugar tongs took Lily back to the days of her own childhood, when her nanny had taught her proper manners by having little tea parties with her. She could almost taste the strawberry jam pennies they had always served. Unlike her own mother, who never participated in the tea parties, Lily promised herself to have jam pennies with her own daughter one day.

Beside the dining area, a completely furnished parlor demanded attention, with its settee, rocker, and two chairs upholstered in velvet. On the center of the settee was a bisque head doll, costumed in a pale pink dress, cloak, and ruched lace cap. Her kid body had been jointed at the hips and arms, and she had eyes that closed, and a woven wig of real hair. She would be the prize of any little girl's doll collection, Lily concluded, thinking of the doll named Emily which she had cherished in her youth.

Behind the parlor was a bedroom with a miniature hammock, a cradle occupied by a baby doll, a chiffonier, a doll swing, and a folding doll rocker of hardwood with an attractive burgundy velvet seat. She set the baby doll in the rocker and gave it a push, smiling at the thought that some day her own little one would find amusement this way.

The last room in the playhouse was a music room, and here Lily played a few notes each on the toy violin, and the toy phonoharp that had twenty-five strings and six bars. A lacquered toy piano with a music rack, thirteen keys, and turned legs caught her eye, and she even managed to plunk out a recognizable version of "Mary had a Little Lamb," followed by polite applause from Hoyt.

"This is simply too much, Hoyt," Lily happily complained, rising from the piano, where she had knelt to give her recital.

"You've only seen half of it," he reminded her, giving her a nudge toward the boy's play area.

Lily's head moved slowly from side to side as she pondered a wooden box. Evidently impatient for her reaction, Hoyt lifted the cover to reveal dozens of compartments, each filled with a toy tool.

"There's a gouge, planer, nail punch, chisel." Hoyt identified the various items as he lifted them out for Lily to see. "Your son will even have his own hammer, screwdriver, and oil can." His eyes were alight with pride.

"I certainly hope you're planning to teach my son how to use these, because I've never even had a hammer in my hand," Lily warned.

"I'll teach your son, if . . . " Suddenly, the sparkle went out of Hoyt's eyes.

Lily tried to puzzle out what he was thinking. "If you have time? Perhaps you'll have to limit your lessons to the off-season."

Though Hoyt's concern had taken a different direction, he followed Lily's line of reasoning. "Yes. Your boy could learn a lot . . . during the winter." He didn't voice the possibility that she might marry someone who would object to his coming around. The very thought was nearly enough to keep him tongue-tied, but he decided he would allow no such affliction to spoil his pleasure this evening, and turned his attention elsewhere.

"This is my favorite toy," he said, picking up a replica of a sidewheel steamer. "It even works!" He turned the sidewheels to show her, his smile returning.

Lily took the boat from him, noticing how closely it resembled the *Lily Belle*. "All it needs is my name on the side and a perfectly wonderful captain, and it will be just like the real thing."

In the next awkward moment, Hoyt recognized the sincerity in Lily's voice, and the fact that her compliment raised questions and feelings better left alone. He took the boat from her and set it aside, pulling her by the elbow to inspect another of his favorite playthings.

Though Lily wanted to tell Hoyt she had never known anyone so big-hearted, thoughtful, kind, and capable, she did not want to intrude on Hoyt's fun. Such genuine com-

85

pliments would have to wait for a more serious discussion.

Hoyt knelt on the floor beside a three foot long oval track which held an iron train. It was nickel plated and consisted of an engine, tender, and passenger coach. "I'd never ride a train, but they make good toys," he explained, pushing the vehicle halfway around the track.

"I appreciate your freedom from bias, at least where toys are concerned," Lily teased, kneeling beside him to take the train the rest of the way around. Bringing it to a stop, she lifted the engine off the track to take a closer look. A cow catcher extended out front, and a stack, valve, and whistle protruded from the top. Though the finish had been buffed, remnants of scratches remained in the nickel. "Was this yours as a child, Hoyt?"

He nodded.

Lily placed it carefully on the track again. "You should keep it for your own son someday."

Though his half-smile remained in place, she could see tension in his jaw. Silent moments lapsed.

Hoyt thought he had learned to control the resentful feelings from his childhood, but seeing the toy train again after all these years was causing old nightmares to resurface.

"Hoyt?" Lily said his name for the third time, then passed her hand in front of his face, which seemed to be set in stone.

He shook his head slightly and unlocked his jaw, though his mouth remained closed. His look was a question.

"I said, maybe you should keep the train for your own son someday."

Hoyt ran his tongue inside his teeth to get his mouth working again. "No need."

Lily wanted to ask for further explanation. Did he mean to imply he would never have a son? Never marry? Such questions would have to wait, for Hoyt had already abandoned the train set for a top, which he had set to spinning in the center of the room.

Beneath the window at the far wall stood a magnificent rocking horse painted like those of a carousel. Lily had gone there to admire the fine workmanship when something soft hit her in the back, then dropped to the floor. She turned to find a cotton-stuffed cloth ball, and a look of devilish merriment in Hoyt's eye.

"Now you've done it," Lily warned, but her return throw was not nearly so accurate.

"We'll see," he said, managing to catch the ball by stretching far to his right. Then he gently pelted her with that ball, and five more like it in rapid succession.

She fended them off with her hands and arms, laughing so hard she went weak in the knees. Her faltering steps brought Hoyt to her side in a flash. Only his steadying arm about her waist kept her from joining the balls on the floor.

"I . . . I'm sorry," Hoyt apologized.

Lily's laughter ceased when she saw Hoyt's look of panic. "Don't worry so. I'm fine," she claimed, though not yet ready to stand alone.

He studied her, unbelieving. "You're p . . . p . . . pale . . . and . . . you look tired," he managed, silently cursing his stubborn tongue.

Before she realized his intention, Hoyt had scooped Lily into his arms and begun carrying her toward the door.

"Captain Curtiss, put me down this instant," she demanded. "I haven't even had a chance to look at all your gifts yet. There's a whole shelf of children's books in the corner to browse." When her plea had no effect, she craned her neck toward the boy's play area and pointed. "Isn't that a toy steam engine? Please show me how it works."

He paused at the top of the stairs to look back, then began his descent to the second floor. "Another time. You need rest."

When he reached the nursery, he carried her to the rocker before setting her down, only to have her pop to her feet, her strength evidently restored.

He put out a staying hand. "I'll see myself out. You get some sleep. It's getting late." He turned to leave.

"You can't go!" she blurted out, not knowing why. She only knew that something inside told her they had much more to say to each other. Her thoughts scrambling, she added, "You can't just shower me with roomsful of expensive gifts, then walk out as if nothing's changed. I can't keep them, you know."

His face went suddenly grim, and a devastated look overtook his features before he drew a mask of nonchalance in place. "So be it. Good night, Lily." He headed out the door.

Had she been a cursing woman, Lily would have turned the air blue scolding herself. How could she have been so unthinking?

"Hoyt, wait!"

CHAPTER
7

Lily hurried after Hoyt, catching him by the arm when he was halfway across her bedroom.

He never slowed, continuing into the upstairs hall.

"I'm sorry, Hoyt. Really. I didn't think. You've been too kind, and I've been an absolute wretch in return. Please forgive me."

At the top of the front stairs, he turned to face her, his emotionless expression unchanged. "I forgive you. Good-bye."

His words sounded flat, unconvincing, but at least he hadn't stammered. How he regretted his lack of an agile tongue.

He made his feet work, instead, carrying him down the stairs to the rhythm of the hurt, angry thoughts that raced through his mind so fast and loud he was barely aware of Lily as she followed him out the front door.

Somewhere on the front walk she gave up, and he continued down the hill alone in his misery. How he had prayed this nightmare would not come to pass.

Absorbed in his own thoughts, he took no notice of his surroundings until he had reached his cabin and was sitting at his desk, his journal open.

July 21, 1897

Lily pleased with gifts. Says she can't keep them. I feel like I have a propeller churning up my insides.

He capped his pen and checked the chronometer on his

desk. The hour read 23:45. He stepped outside. Mad Jack was not in sight. He must be enjoying Agatha's company. At least something was going well this evening. Hoyt watched the light on the south pierhead sending its beam across the lake into inky blackness. Clouds had moved in to blot out stars and moon and drop a shroud of fog over the shoreline.

Tomorrow the haze would burn off, and perhaps the propeller tearing his gut apart would run out of steam.

Disheartened, Lily watched Hoyt disappear into the darkness, then turned toward the house. She had never seen him so distressed, and she had only herself to blame for losing control of her errant tongue. Why could she never learn to think before speaking?

She crossed the veranda and let herself inside, meeting up with Margaret who was hastily pushing a baby carriage through the front hall. Lily started up the stairs, hoping to avoid an encounter, but relented when she heard the note of urgency in the maid's voice.

"Your captain's gone then, is he, ma'am? I was meaning to show you this so's you could thank him before he got away."

Lily relented, turning back from the second step. "Yes, Margaret, he's gone." Disappointment overshadowed the note of frustration in her reply. She glanced at the reed conveyance with its woven cane webbing, silk lining, and fine satin parasol with a wide lace edge, and felt even more miserable than before. "I shall be sure and thank him for the baby carriage," she promised.

Continuing up the stairs, she dreaded the knowledge that everywhere would be reminders of the disaster the evening had become. In her room, she folded the flannel apparel and

90

linens on her bed, put them away in her dresser, and pulled back the coverlet and sheet.

All the while she was unhooking her dress, removing her petticoat, and trading her camisole for her white silk nightgown, she could think only of how insensitive she had been in the face of Hoyt's generosity.

She doused her light and stretched out on her horsehair mattress, a cooling breeze ruffling the lacy window curtains. Fatigued but not sleepy, she lay there on her back, eyes wide open and knees bent. Her mind returned again and again to the pained look on Hoyt's face when she had said she couldn't keep his gifts. For one instant, he had looked utterly crestfallen! She turned on her side and forced her lids shut, but the image seemed even sharper, and she felt as tight as an overwound clock.

How she wished Aunt Agatha were there to talk to. Giving up the quest for sleep, she wandered into the nursery and sat in the wicker rocking chair, gently rocking back and forth while awaiting her aunt's return. She heard Margaret come up the back stairs to her servant's quarters, and the clock on the downstairs mantel chime midnight . . . a quarter past . . . half past . . .

Still no closer to sleep, she fetched from her bottom dresser drawer the half completed embroidery of Mackinac Island that she had not worked on since Parker's accident, and returned to the rocker to stitch. One o'clock came, and then two.

The breeze picked up. Thunder rumbled in the distance. Gusts of wind brought the smell of rain into the room. Huge droplets spattered against the nursery window and Lily rushed to close it, and the one in her own room. Already, it was nearly three o'clock.

Where was Agatha?

Moments after the rain began, Lily heard the sound of shuffling footsteps and a cane on the front stair treads. Setting embroidery aside, she rushed to assist her aunt.

"Where on earth have you been? Do you realize how late it is? I've been worried about you!"

"Surely Captain Curtiss told you I was going out for a drive with Jack," Agatha answered perfunctorily. "I'd still be with him if it weren't for the dratted storm."

Helping her aunt up the last step, Lily scolded, "But it's past three o'clock!"

Agatha tapped her cane on the floor. "See here, young lady. I know very well how late it is. I've been able to tell time for at least sixty-five years."

"You should have come home hours ago," Lily insisted, leading Agatha by the arm to the southeast bedroom.

The elderly woman came to an abrupt halt outside her door. "What the devil has put you in such a snit, girl? I'd have thought you'd be happy for me. After all, this has been my first night to enjoy the company of a gentleman since dearly departed Wilbur went to his final resting place ten years ago. And here you stand, scolding me for taking some innocent pleasure in a drive with a lonely widower. I can't for the life of me understand you, niece. Weren't you pleased with Captain Curtiss's surprise?"

"Of course I was pleased! That has nothing—" Suddenly, Lily realized her problems with Hoyt had everything to do with her present state. Impetuously, she hugged Agatha. "I'm sorry. Really I am. You're absolutely right. I'm behaving abominably. It's just that—" Lily bit her lip, wondering how to explain.

"It's just that *what*?" Agatha took Lily by the hand and led her into her room. Using her cane as a pointer, she ordered, "Sit."

Lily sat in the Windsor chair as commanded, and her aunt took another chair beside her. "Now, talk. I want to know how you came to be in such a state."

Starting slowly, Lily described her evening from the moment she had entered the house, her words spilling out as she told about the discoveries she shared with Hoyt in the playroom. Her tongue danced quickly to Hoyt's leavetaking. "So I said, 'You can't just shower me with gifts, then walk out as if nothing's changed,' and when he kept on going, I said, 'I can't keep them, you know.'"

A look of horror crossed Agatha's face. "Lily, how *could* you?"

"I don't know why I said it. Maybe I thought it would keep him from leaving—get him to talk to me—if only to argue the point."

Agatha's head moved slowly from side to side. "'A slip of the foot you may soon recover, but a slip of the tongue you may never get over.'" Agatha quoted Franklin, then clucked her tongue. "Lily, you've much to learn about a man's pride. It's far more fragile than a woman's. I'd liken it to a tower built of straw. From outward appearances, it's a mighty thing, but a puff of wind can take it down. Your words hit with hurricane force.

"What's worse, when you said you couldn't keep the gifts, you were rejecting more than the presents, you were rejecting the man himself. He probably inferred that they just aren't good enough for you. And to think *I* encouraged him in this scheme. Whatever must he think of me now?"

"Auntie, you've got to help me. How can I show Hoyt I'm really sorry, that I didn't mean what I said about returning the gifts?"

"You'll have to go talk to him—the sooner, the better—and hope he'll allow you back into his good graces."

Lily chewed on her knuckle, then a look of hope smoothed the worry lines on her forehead. "I've got it. I'll see him first thing in the morning, before the excursion run to Ottawa Beach, and ask him if I may have the pleasure of his company at luncheon in the private dining room on board the *Lily Belle*. I'll have the chef prepare his favorite foods." The ominous sound of thunder rumbled just overhead. "I'd prefer a picnic at the beach, but I'm afraid the weather won't cooperate."

"Sounds like a good idea. I'm planning to take the *Lily Belle* to Ottawa Beach myself. Jack invited me."

Lily drew a quick breath. "I forgot to ask about your evening with Captain Jack."

Agatha's pale blue eyes twinkled. "Just fine, my dear. It was wonderful, remembering old times. That is, until the rain came." She gave a look of disdain.

"I'm glad you enjoyed each other's company." Lily yawned. "I suppose I ought to try and get some rest. Morning light will come too soon, I'm afraid."

"Good night, Lily."

Though the rain had stopped for the time being, dismal, dark clouds prevented the morning sun from brightening Lily's room as she prepared for the excursion to Ottawa Beach. Neither did the black merino dress she pulled on over her camisole and petticoat do anything to enliven her spirits.

She was probably the last person Hoyt wanted to see this morning. Regardless, she resolutely fixed her black straw boater in place on her head with two combs and a five-inch jet hat pin, claimed her umbrella from the stand in the hallway, and stepped off at a brisk pace toward the dock.

A cool, damp breeze tested her hat, bringing with it the

essence of Unger's fish market. At a little past eight, the waterfront was still sleepy, except for a few small fishing craft and the ever present sea gulls calling to one another. Lily had specifically chosen this quiet time, two hours before her ship's departure, to approach Hoyt.

Before she had even decided what to say to him, she had reached the *Lily Belle*, and with some trepidation, she boarded via the gangplank. In the main lounge, a steward was straightening chairs and wiping table tops. She sent him for Hoyt, then waited apprehensively by the window that overlooked the south side of town, watching a hack make its way along Water Street.

When the young attendant returned to say Hoyt would soon join her, she explained her need to speak to the captain confidentially and tipped him generously to ensure privacy. A minute later, her captain's expansive shoulders more than filled the doorway, requiring him to turn slightly sideways as he entered. She forced a smile, noticing his careworn look, and wondered whether he had slept at all.

"Good morning, Captain." She left the window niche to stand nearer him by the stack casing, twisting the umbrella nervously in her hands.

Despite Hoyt's long, troubled night, spent for the most part without sleep, he was truly glad to see Lily. Her usually bright eyes showed more than a touch of weariness, and her smile was unmistakably subdued, but he felt some sense of relief now that she was really here.

"Good morning, Mrs. Haynes." He removed his cap.

Lily simply looked at him for a long moment, taking measure of the kindness in his almost-smile, the gentle strength in the pair of rough, wide hands that fidgeted with his hat, and the compassion evident in his eyes, though they were red-rimmed with fatigue.

She drew in a fortifying breath. "I've decided to sail with you to Ottawa Beach this morning and I was wondering whether you would agree to luncheon with me in the private dining room?"

Hoyt found himself nodding before Lily had even finished the invitation that came out in a rush. "Yes. Thank you." He wanted to say so much more, but he trusted his tongue only that far.

She was visibly relieved. "Good. Wonderful. I'll tell the chef." She nearly floated from the room, turning back once to reveal a much happier smile.

Lily's conversation with the chef was both brief and specific. She requested only that he prepare Hoyt's favorite dish for them both, not even inquiring what that might be, and from her head waiter, she asked for service for two in the private dining room at noon. Then she returned home to make certain her aunt had risen and was prepared for the day-long outing to the port that lay about an hour by steamer north of South Haven.

While her aunt was finishing her toilet, Lily went to her own room and removed the Samuel Ward Stanton drawing from her wall, allowing access to the small safe behind. Opening the combination lock, she took out a tiny velvet box and slipped it into her skirt pocket.

An hour before the ship's departure, Jack Wilson came to fetch Agatha and Lily to the dock. The ladies were quite impressed with the grand Cunningham carriage he drove. It hung low, permitting easy access for women, and its body was intricately hand carved with a diamond pattern, giving it a look of distinction. The braces and steps were silver plated, and the interior had been finished in navy blue tufted leather and velvet upholstery.

Cunningham carriages, built in Rochester, New York, were among the finest money could buy, and in the past two years had achieved quite a reputation among the well-to-do back East, but until now, Lily hadn't seen one in the Midwest.

The pair of matched grays that drew them smartly along Erie Street, then down the Maple Street hill to the river, had been groomed to perfection, and Lily couldn't help wondering where the old Lake Michigan man had come upon such a fine team.

Aboard the *Lily Belle*, Lily had planned to leave Jack and Agatha to their own company. But when the old captain insisted he needed a new audience for his stories of the good old days on the lakes, then launched into such colorful tales as the time he shot a pigeon and discovered it to be smuggling a diamond stud from Canada into the United States, she found him too entertaining to resist.

In no time, it seemed, the *Lily Belle* was nearing Ottawa Beach, and Lily left the elderly couple comfortably seated on a sofa in the lounge to watch the approach from the deck. At a distance, the pierheads bore similarity to those at South Haven, with the light on the southern arm of the channel connected by a long catwalk to the beach.

Once in the channel, the resort-like nature of the waterfront became more obvious. Though the Ottawa Beach Hotel, stretching along the northern shore, had been visible from a distance, Lily now caught a better view of the jutting roof line and long series of arched openings that distinguished this expansive hostelry which had been built to accommodate a thousand guests.

The opposite side of the channel, in contrast with this sprawling resort, was Macatawa Park, its sandy shore lined with trees and greenery.

The *Lily Belle* tied up at the resort hotel's dock, which enjoyed excellent rail service offering connections with the cities of Holland and Grand Rapids. Such access made the port a popular one for her passengers, even on a cloudy, sometimes rainy day like this one.

The Ottawa was being run by Mr. Rathbone, of the Morton House in Grand Rapids. He had acquired such a fine reputation for his establishments, Lily was not surprised that Captain Jack had offered to take Agatha there for luncheon. She saw them off the *Lily Belle*, then headed to the private dining room on board to meet Hoyt.

He did not keep her waiting, but was ready to go in when she arrived outside the mahogany paneled door. Inside, the room was finished in pleasing tones of beige and pale green above knotted pine paneling, and featured oil paintings of natural scenes in lower Michigan including the sand dunes along the Lake Michigan shoreline, the huge white pines that had existed in great forests before falling to the lumberman's axe, and the Grand Ledge, a unique rock formation located in the interior of the state.

Hoyt seated her at the round table that had been spread with a fine white damask cloth. The waiter served a first course of apple juice, followed by clear consommé, then salad greens dressed in oil and vinegar.

Conversation was polite, but restrained, with Lily carrying the bulk of it on such neutral topics as the unveiling of the equestrian statue of General John A. Logan two days earlier in Chicago's Lake Front Park, and the parade of nineteen thousand men afterward to celebrate the event.

The main course arrived on covered plates. Lily was expecting the waiter to reveal filet mignon or some equally beefy entrée, but was delighted to discover Welsh rarebit instead.

She waited for the attendant to leave the room before getting to the reason for their luncheon.

Laying her fork down, she looked directly into Hoyt's eyes. "About last night. I'm terribly sorry for the way things ended. I didn't mean what I said. I know I hurt you deeply, and there's no excuse for such abominable behavior. It's just that," a hint of a smile teased at her mouth, "unlike you, I seem to have very little control over my tongue. It just wags on and on and words come pouring out of my mouth faster than my brain can even think them up!"

His brown eyes were fastened on her, neither condemning nor accepting, and in the awkwardness of the next moment's silence, she wondered what must be going through Hoyt's mind. She glanced down at her plate and fidgeted with her spoon, too unsettled to eat.

Then he lifted her chin with one finger and told her in that quiet, mellow voice of his, "I understand."

Their gazes locked, and they exchanged a look that surpassed words.

She laid her spoon aside and reached into her skirt pocket. Against the stark white tablecloth, she placed the midnight blue velvet box. "For you, Hoyt. Please accept it as a token of my thanks for the baby carriage, and all the other gifts you gave me last night."

He wanted to refuse, but as usual, his tongue was slow to take up the thoughts his shaking head conveyed, and Lily strengthened her argument.

"Parker would be pleased for you to have, and wear these," she said, popping open the lid to reveal an elegant pair of gold cuff links inscribed with the ship's insignia. "He had them custom engraved by Mr. Hylen on Dearborn Street. There are no others like them in all the world, and you should have them."

He cradled the box in his hand, a look of great compassion on his face as he admired its contents, and Lily could only guess that he was remembering the sad loss of his friend.

Hoyt closed the box and found a place for it inside his breast pocket close to his heart, the heart that had been so badly broken last night, and was healing so nicely this noon. "Thank you, Lily. I—I—"

"You'll wear them in good health," she finished for him.

He had meant to say he was glad she had decided to keep his gifts, but he nodded agreement to her own version of his unspoken words. He worked his tongue around in his mouth, and raised a finger as if ready to speak, hoping his next thoughts would emerge as intended. "Lily, I want you to know I—I—" Drat! He prayed he wouldn't go scarlet with embarrassment.

Lily waited quietly, for once, for him to continue.

He inhaled deeply, determined to say his piece straight through. "I want you to know I will always be ready to help you, no matter what." To that, he wanted to add that he cared a great deal for her, but no good could come of such an admission to a widow of a mere two and a half months. She needed time, and he was a patient man.

Lily had sensed that Hoyt was on the verge of some significant revelation, but his admission was not surprising. She was afraid to reveal, however, that her feelings for him had exceeded those of a ship owner for her captain, sailing swiftly into the deeper waters of fondness and caring. Giving air to such sentiments would only make for rough going. She must choose her words carefully, keeping them genuine, but light.

"Hoyt, any man who is as generous with a woman as you were with me last night, has already let his actions speak for his feelings, but it's nice to hear the words, too."

He gave a quick nod, harboring the acute frustration of an inept tongue.

The waiter returned to clear the dishes from the main course. When he served dessert, Lily was glad Hoyt's preference ran to fresh blueberries and cream rather than rich Black Forest torte, or sinfully fattening cheesecake.

She was on her second mouthful of the sweet, plump berries when Hoyt set his spoon aside and leaned slightly forward.

"Lily, you said earlier ... you said you don't have c ... c ... control of your tongue like me. Well, you're not ... you're not quite right." A smile crept across his face. "Truth is, I ... I don't have control of my tongue, either!"

She immediately caught his meaning, unable to suppress a grin, or the giggle that bubbled up in the back of her throat. Hoyt, too, began to chuckle, so infectiously, they soon shared gales of laughter.

When the hilarity had subsided, she dabbed a tear from the corner of her eye and pronounced, "We're a perfect match. Can you imagine what would happen if we both talked as much as I do, or as little as you?"

Her hypothesis led to renewed laughter, and several moments passed before they were able to again take up their spoons. By the time they had finished with dessert, a more subdued atmosphere had returned, and while sipping a second glass of milk, Hoyt told Lily in his own halting way about his childhood.

As he did, he could still hear his father lecturing him to stay away from the docks when he was a boy of five, and feel the rush of fear at the threat of a whipping. It was as if he were catapulted backward in time to one of the countless Friday nights when Carlton Curtiss, an engineer for the

101

Illinois Central, came home from a week of riding the rails to reacquaint himself with wife and children.

Unfortunately, he always made a stop at the tavern, and after four hours of drinking whiskey, he would arrive home in an abusive disposition.

Before he had even removed his engineer's cap from his head, Carlton would be blaming his wife, Ada, for an unkept house, bad cooking, and slovenly personal appearance. Sadly, Ada Curtiss deserved none of these criticisms, but in her husband's altered state, he imagined she did and berated her mercilessly.

When Hoyt was young, he ran from the small house and hid in the woodshed, but in later years, he would defend his mother, bringing upon himself a flow of deriding remarks designed to remind him that he would never amount to anything.

These encounters had left deep emotional scars, including Hoyt's stammer and his extreme dislike of anything connected with the railroad. His dread of repeating the travesty with a son of his own was another lingering concern, though irrational since he never touched alcohol.

He did not explain how the problem with his speech had caused such enormous feelings of inadequacy that he had always felt the need to prove himself through his actions, and how action was the crutch upon which he often relied to give voice to his feelings.

But Lily was an intelligent woman, and she would probably make the connection between his stammer, and his sometimes extravagant conduct, on her own.

Despite the congeniality shared over the luncheon in the private dining room, discretion ruled their behavior when Hoyt and Lily emerged into the main lobby. With barely a parting word or glance, he resumed his duties in the pilothouse and she returned to the main lounge to await Jack and Agatha's return.

For the next several days, Jack Wilson sailed constantly on the *Lily Belle*, helping to analyze performance of machinery and crew, making suggestions for improvements of their operation. Though the steamer increased her efficiency, making better time on each run, the *Huron Queen* seemed somehow to improve at the same pace, running neck and neck, claiming the best time between ports as often as her competitor.

When the *Lily Belle* was in South Haven, Jack's frequent visits to the Queen Anne home on the corner of Erie and St. Joseph Streets kept Agatha in an unusually cheerful state, besides causing her to take serious inventory of her wardrobe, to the point of ordering from the seamstress three new dresses in various shades of purple!

Lily sent a copy of the race rules to Alick as promised, and followed Jack's advice to make the most of pre-race publicity by sending letters to the editors of both the *Sentinel* in South Haven and the *Tribune* in Chicago, notifying them of the event.

Though she had expected an article to appear in each publication, she was shocked by the headlines that appeared in the *Tribune* the week before the race.

CHAPTER
8

HURON QUEEN CHALLENGES
LILY BELLE TO RACE

A. L. Haynes, owner of the Haynes Transit Company, who now has the D & C Line steamer *Huron Queen* under charter, has challenged the Sweetwater Steamship Line's *Lily Belle* to a race from Chicago to South Haven, the route on which the two vessels have been competing for the lucrative passenger and freight traffic for several days.

Haynes denied that the challenge to race resulted in any way from the recent change in management of the *Lily Belle*, over which he was once superintendent. This ship is now under management of Mrs. Lily Haynes, widow of Alick Haynes' brother, Parker . . .

Lily slapped the paper against her hand and paced back and forth in front of Hoyt, who was sitting casually, foot on knee, at the oak library table in the center of the room. "How could they print such a lie?" she asked angrily, red blotches spreading over her cheeks. "I'm going right to the editor's office on Tuesday and set him straight."

Hoyt disliked upsetting Lily, in her condition, but he knew she would learn about the article soon enough, and he'd just as soon be there when she did. Besides, he had a plan for calming her trigger temper.

"I've already set him straight," he stated calmly.

Lily stopped abruptly to face him, her blond brows meeting in disbelief. "You have?"

Hoyt's head dipped.

"You walked into his office, grabbed him by the collar, and demanded he print the truth?" she questioned.

Hoyt chuckled. "He promised to correct the story in tomorrow's paper."

"It's the very least he can do," she said in a huff.

An accurate version of the story ran the following day, including apologies for the previous day's misinformation. Hoyt did not tell Lily that he had managed such favorable treatment by threatening to discontinue selling the *Tribune* from the *Lily Belle's* newsstand.

During the remaining days before the race, Lily was busy setting final plans in place for officials and stakeboats at the finish line, and obtaining government patrol boats to prevent interference along the course by other vessels.

Little more was printed about the subject until the day before the race, when the *Tribune* ran a story very similar to the large spread in South Haven's *Sentinel*.

THE SENTINEL

Volume LVI Number 217   August 5, 1897   South Haven

LILY BELLE FIT FOR BIG RACE

MANAGER LILY HAYNES SAYS FLYER IS

IN SPLENDID CONDITION.

FIVE BOATS LEAVE DETROIT FOR THE GREAT CONTEST.

LILY BELLE HAS SHIPPED SIXTY TONS OF HANDPICKED COAL.

ENGINES WORKED IN EASY STYLE IN YESTERDAY'S RUN.

LILY BELLE FIT FOR GREAT RACE.

Mrs. Lily Haynes, manager of the Sweetwater Line, said last night:

"Nothing we could do has been left undone . . .

Detroit to Send Big Crowd.

Detroit, August 4- The steamer *City of Detroit* will go down the lake twenty miles beyond the stakeboat, returning with the racers . . .

Interest at Benton Harbor/St. Joe

Benton Harbor, August 4 - About 200 people have bought tickets to go out on the ferry *Grace Ann* . . .

Great Interest at Chicago

Chicago, August 4 - Steamboat men from all parts of the country will come here to see the contest . . .

Both Are Side Wheelers.

Both steamers were designed and built by Frank Kirby, undisputably the foremost designer of lake steamers . . .

Wagers Placed

A number of wagers at even money have been made . . . the largest of which was $1,000 . . . the betting has been lively over the last several days . . .

Patrol Boats for the Race.

Patrol boats will be designated by a white flag with a black letter P in the center and all other boats will be kept clear of the racing lines . . .

Rules of the Race.

The conditions of the race follow:
1. Race time and date . . .
2. The course to be . . .
3. Stakeboats shall mark beginning and ending . . .
4. Judges shall be disinterested parties . . .
5. Timekeepers shall be selected . . .
6. Searchers shall see that the steamers maintain parallel courses . . .
7. Starting positions shall be decided by lot . . .
8. Inspectors shall be on board each steamer . . .

9. Postponement in case of bad weather or rough water . . .

10. The $2,000 shall be forfeited in case of either party . . .

11. All expenses shall be borne equally by the parties signing this agreement . . .

12. All questions shall be referred to the judges and their decision shall be final.

While the newspapers made public much of the information regarding the race, reporters were unaware of the preparations going on behind the scenes. Though the *Lily Belle* carried her usual load of passengers and freight into South Haven on Thursday evening, under cover of darkness, Hoyt and his crew made hasty changes.

Stewards stowed lifeboats and flagpoles on the lower deck to reduce wind resistance, while the engine room crew installed new piston rings and built a wooden bulkhead around the steamer condenser. This box, ten feet square and six feet deep, would be filled with cracked ice in Chicago just before the start of the race. Captain Jack had determined that by lowering the temperature of the condenser, they would be able to increase the power of the engine. He also requested the engineer to slack off all the bearings to reduce friction.

Just as Hoyt, Jack, and the crew of the *Lily Belle* were making ready for the great race, Lily and Agatha considered preparations for a party, hopefully a victory celebration for all involved, to be held at her home on the hill after the finish line had been crossed. Ridgley had come from Chicago to assist Margaret in planning and serving the fish boil, fresh sweet corn, watermelon and cantaloupe, and all manner of blueberry breads, muffins, pies and cobblers.

Gallons of sweet lemonade, Lily's favorite summertime beverage, were made from dozens of fresh lemons, and plenty of ice for chilling the drink was ordered from the ice man.

Blue and white bunting—the colors of the Sweetwater Steamship Line—was hung at the front of the veranda, and lanterns of the same colors were attached to the overhang of the wide porch as well. The *Lily Belle's* china and flatware were brought from her kitchen to serve guests. Picnic tables were arranged from panels laid atop sawhorses, and benches consisted of boards upon empty kegs, compliments of Snowhill's lumber yard where the *Lily Belle* leased her dock space.

Though preparations continued far into the night, Lily went up to her room at half past twelve on the eve of the race, knowing that to stay up any later would be to risk rising on time for the departure. While brushing her hair and readying herself for bed, she thought of the significance of the race and the irony of it.

The winner would undoubtedly have all the traffic she could handle. The loser . . . would she even be able to continue in the shipping business, Lily wondered? In the flurry of excitement she had not given thought to the possibility of losing. Her confidence in Hoyt and her entire crew had been high, and she had not considered such an eventuality.

Parker had held lofty standards for the *Lily Belle*, and she would not see them diminished. Before turning out her light, she knew she would rise a little earlier than planned, and do what she could to inspire her crew to victory.

The day dawned partly sunny with a gusty wind from the southwest. Four-foot waves broke against the pierheads and the sandy shoreline, but all in all, it looked like a fair day for a race.

Agatha was bright-eyed and ready for the outing, spurred on, in part, Lily thought, by the prospect of a day spent in the company of Jack Wilson. He had finally succumbed to pressures to make use of Lily's guest bedroom, where he had been staying for the past week, though he claimed he had only moved off Hoyt's couch because it gave him backaches.

Agatha had been in her glory, doting on him when he was in the house, which wasn't often, so devoted was he to his responsibility to guide Hoyt and the *Lily Belle* to victory. He had, in fact, spent most of last night on the ship, as near as Lily could determine, for he had gone to the docks hours before she and Agatha arrived at eight A.M.

For safety reasons, passengers were not permitted aboard during the race, but Lily, Agatha, and Jack signed on as additional members of the crew, and so did some distinguished South Haven residents such as Mr. Pettish, editor of *The Sentinel*, and Dr. Adams, the town physician.

When all were aboard who planned to sail, Lily assembled her entire crew in the main lounge to hear her words of inspiration.

"I wish Parker were here to speak to you today," she began. "He was so much better than I at giving encouragement.

"Thinking about him last night, I realized he would want to make clear certain points before the start of the race. First, he would thank you for the service you have given the *Lily Belle* thus far. He would have been pleased with the record she has established. Her success represents a fulfillment of his dream to run the finest passenger and freight liner on Lake Michigan!

"I think you'll agree that Parker believed in treating you

with fairness, respect and dignity, because he believed, as I do, that every decent individual deserves nothing less. When he was on board, he made a point of showing a personal interest in you. You demonstrated your appreciation for his caring by welcoming him into your presence each time he sailed with you, and by your outpouring of sympathy after his . . . accident. He knew he could count on you to give your finest efforts.

"As for the race, he would ask you to continue to do your best . . . not for him, but for yourselves. You see, no one knows what lies ahead for the loser of this competition. Perhaps she could continue to sail with lighter loads each trip, perhaps not.

"Our future, yours and mine, might very well be tied up in the outcome of today's competition. If the *Lily Belle* is forced off this lake, a part of Parker will go with her. I ask you . . . *please* don't let that happen. He loved this ship. He cherished you, his crew." Her voice faded to a half-whisper. *"Don't let Parker's dream die!"*

Were it not for the plush carpet covering the floor, Lily could have heard a pin drop, the lounge was so silent as she left the room.

Emerging alone on the promenade deck, she leaned against the rail, adjusting her straw boater against the cool, gusty breeze that rustled the leaves, sent a gull soaring on an updraft, and carried to her the trace of smoked fish. She lifted her eyes to her house on the hill, and worked at dissolving the lump which had settled in her throat.

She had thought her moments of profound grief over Parker were all in the past. Now, she realized his memory would always be with her, and she was thankful for the new way in which she was able to think of him.

No longer was she resentful over the amount of time he

had devoted to his ship and the lack of attention he had paid her. Their marriage had been so short, she didn't look back on him so much as the one she had wed, but as a man with a vision. By becoming his wife, she had been able to share his plans. How long it had taken her to appreciate them!

Love had been a part of it all. Parker's for her, and hers for him, but these feelings now dwelt in their own special place, not overshadowing other emotions, as they had in the aftermath of his accident.

Near the bow, Hoyt was resting an elbow on the rail, observing her. The sun broke through a cloud, brightening his kind but rugged face and his well-groomed navy wool uniform with its brassy braid and buttons. Her mouth pulled into a smile. She felt drawn to him to share her most recent discoveries about herself and the man they both had cared for so deeply, but this was not the time.

Touching a finger to his visor, the captain dipped his head and turned to climb the stairs to the pilothouse.

A whiff of bay rum tinged the air, and Lily knew even before he joined her at the rail that Captain Jack had emerged from the lounge. A look of respect emanated from his clear hazel eyes. "'Twas quite a speech you gave in there, my girl. I believe every last man on your crew right down to the coal passers would jump through flaming hoops for you, Lily."

She chuckled softly. "You think so?"

"I'm convinced of it."

"They needn't do anything so foolish. All I ask is that they do their jobs, *especially* the coal passers. Without them, we'll be dead in the water!"

"That would never happen."

Lily gazed into the face of the man whose salt and pepper beard gave him the look of a seaworthy Solomon.

"Who do you really believe will win this race?"

He scratched his chin and squinted at her. "Alick has more experienced officers. They're older, a bit more savvy. Your crew, on the other hand, is greener, younger. But they love working for you, and they've got enthusiasm. You know I'm not a betting man, but my $500 says the *Lily Belle* will take the prize."

Lily nearly choked. "Five hundred dollars?"

He nodded decisively.

"How can you be so certain about the outcome?"

He tapped a finger on her arm. "Even if the *Huron Queen* crosses the finish line first, your ship is a winner."

She shook her head vigorously. "How can you say that?"

"I've been listening to people who have booked passage on both steamers. They tell me traveling the *Lily Belle* is more fun because the crew seems to enjoy their work more. The atmosphere is pleasant, the stewards and stewardesses are more friendly.

"Alick may have a slick ship and more experienced officers, but the men below decks are inexperienced, and he doesn't respect them. He drives them for every ounce of flesh he can get, and pays them only what's necessary to keep them at their posts.

"I doubt he'll win the competition, but if he does, I don't think you'll suffer loss of traffic. You already have a loyal clientele." He winked. "But I'm glad you didn't know that when you gave your speech." He left her to join Agatha, who had taken a deck chair near the bow.

Lily felt a bit overwhelmed by Jack's appraisal, and a trifle relieved, but she was not yet confident enough in the outcome of the contest to put aside all her worries.

As the *Lily Belle* steamed toward Chicago, talk among

both her regular and special crew members often centered on the wagers which had been made on the outcome of the race. Agatha admitted to placing a hefty one on the *Lily Belle*, but would not divulge the amount.

As for the $1,000 put up for charity, Hoyt had challenged Alick to the race, and had therefore insisted on providing the stake. He had confided to her, though, that he never had gambled before in his life.

Lily hadn't placed any bet at all. She never had believed in gambling.

In Chicago, a crowd had gathered at the *Lily Belle's* dock to greet her when she tied up to take on ice. Lily was warmed by the sight. Since this was not her home port, she could only assume the throng consisted of the loyal clientele to whom Jack had referred.

When the lines were cast off, a thick stream of boats—yachts, sloops, even fishing vessels—followed her down the river onto the lake, many staying with her until turned back by the patrol vessels near the stakeboats that marked the start of the race.

The *Huron Queen* was already making a pass near the starting line, her bow in perfect trim, her decks stripped of unnecessary equipment. A chill passed along Lily's spine as she thought of Alick, ruthless and cunning, at command.

Lots were drawn for choice of position. The *Huron Queen* won and Alick chose the outer position, putting more distance between his boat and the shore, though the advantage was negligible since the course ran a straight line, cutting across open water rather than following the shoreline.

At two P.M., the *Lily Belle* came abreast of the *Huron Queen*. From one of the stakeboats marking the start of the race, a gun was fired and the ships were off, full steam ahead!

CHAPTER
9

With her paddlewheels churning and her smokestack spewing forth great, billowing black clouds, the *Lily Belle* took the lead while Hoyt, Lily, and Jack watched their competition from the port window of the pilothouse. Though the *Huron Queen* was off to a slow start, she was soon running stem and stem with the *Lily Belle*, and within ten minutes, had gained a length on her.

"Captain," Jack began gravely, "with your permission, I'm going below to see how many turns she's doing." He was referring, Lily knew, to the number of revolutions per minute being generated by the steam from the boilers.

Hoyt nodded, his eyes never leaving the *Queen*.

A sense of helplessness washed over Lily as she watched the other boat increase her advantage to three lengths. "I have a feeling this is going to be a very long race," she confided to Hoyt, not wanting the nearby wheelsman and navigator to overhear. With an attempt at optimism, she added, "No matter. We'll come out winners."

Hoyt was silently working his jaw, intent on the *Queen*, but managed to wrest his eyes from the other steamer to take in the fairhaired, black-clad angel by his side, the woman who had captured, then lost one of the best men he had ever counted as a friend. He had been profoundly touched by her tribute to Parker this morning, and he had been reminded that she was, and would for a long time to come, remain a widow in mourning.

Her compelling words had drilled deep into his heart, touching a core of mixed emotions—regret over the loss of Parker, determination to win the race in his honor, respect for a lady plucky enough to go up against one of the toughest shippers in the business. He would not let her down today, or ever.

Looking Lily straight in the eye, he promised, "Tonight, you'll be the victor."

Hoyt's expression was so serious, Lily couldn't resist a try at lightening his mood. She tugged playfully on his beard. "Tonight, we'll all be victors, for simply having lived through this!" She headed toward the stairs. "I'll check on Agatha and leave you to your job. I can keep track of the *Huron Queen* from the lounge just as easily as from up here. Chin up, Captain. We're only another seventy miles or so from the finish line."

In the lounge, Agatha was alternately sipping lemonade and looking through her binoculars at the *Queen*. "She's turning up quite a wake. Good thing she's required to run her course at a half-mile distance, or you'd be eating her backwash." She offered the glasses to her niece.

Lily put palm up. "Her lead is all I care about, and I can see that well enough without the benefit of magnification." She slumped onto a chair, wondering how she'd kept her mask of confidence in place for Hoyt.

"Don't look so discouraged. We've barely gotten started. Anything can happen!" Agatha claimed enthusiastically. Looking over her shoulder, she lowered her voice to a whisper and cupped her hand to Lily's ear. "Better look confident. Here comes Mr. Pettish."

In full morning suit, the tall newspaper editor crossed the room from the table he had been sharing with Dr. Adams, the wide strides of his overly long, thin legs carrying him, uninvited, to the chair beside Lily.

Notebook in hand, pen poised, he spoke in the rapid patter so common to his breed. "Mrs. Haynes, the *Queen*

116

has moved ahead. Any words as to how you're going to win back the lead?"

"Luck and hard work, Mr. Pettish."

In a dash, he'd taken down the quote. Obviously not satisfied, he probed her with his beady dark eyes. "No secret plans for powering up in a pinch?"

Lily offered him her most charming smile, and in her sweetest voice, repeated, "Luck and hard work, Mr. Pettish. Now that you have your quote, you won't mind taking your leave so I can discuss personal matters with my aunt." When he was slow to take the hint, she firmly added, "Thank you, Mr. Pettish. I knew you'd understand."

Though his scowl said she'd regret inviting him to go, he went without further words.

"Persistent fellow, eh?" Agatha muttered under her breath.

"If I didn't need the publicity, I'd have never allowed him aboard," Lily confided.

Over the next several minutes, the *Lily Belle* seemed to edge closer to the *Queen*.

Agatha raised her binoculars again. "I do believe we're going to overtake the competition," she concluded.

The tapping of Jack's cane against the hardwood floor announced his arrival. "You are so right, my dear," he confirmed, pulling a chair close to Agatha and taking her hand in his.

"What did you find below?" Lily asked eagerly. "How did you improve our speed?"

Before he could even answer, Mr. Pettish was by his side, pen poised.

Looking from Pettish to Lily, Jack chuckled. "Guess you're not the only one who wants to know. It was really quite simple. When I checked on the furnaces, I discovered the boys were burning coal from the wrong bunker. They were shoveling in the standard grade, not the hand-picked supply we took on special for the race."

"Shoveling wrong coal," Pettish repeated slowly as his pen put the words to paper.

"That's it," Jack confirmed.

Evidently satisfied, Pettish rushed to share the news at his table.

"Thank goodness you noticed the error," Lily said. Taking up Agatha's glasses, she announced, "I do believe we are about to give the competition a good look at our aft decks."

But such was not to be. For the next half hour the two vessels ran even. Lily ventured to the main port deck. Running at twenty-two miles an hour on the open water made for a very brisk, cold breeze. She slapped warmth into her upper arms and considered climbing to the pilothouse again when she detected a distinct loss of power.

Captain Jack emerged from the main lounge in a rather nimble fashion, considering his arthritic legs, and made swiftly for the passageway that would take him to the engine room.

Meanwhile, the *Queen* again took the lead. Feeling helpless, Lily returned to Agatha's table in the lounge to await word on the status below.

Pettish queried her and was told to wait for Jack's return. Twenty minutes later, when the *Lily Belle* had fallen behind her competition by a good half-mile, she regained her momentum and Jack came above to make his report to both Lily and Pettish, who had appeared on winged feet when the old man entered the room.

"The starboard engine blower failed. We got her going again, but she's not as efficient as she should be," he ex-

118

plained.

"You mean we have to run the rest of this race handicapped by a malfunctioning blower?" Lily quickly asked, successfully edging out Pettish in a quest for further explanation.

"No choice. Can't fix her proper 'till we're in port."

"There's your news of the hour, Mr. Pettish," Lily said pointedly. Evidently satisfied, the newsman took his leave. Sighing hugely, she said to Jack, "I guess I should be thankful you've been able to fix it at all, but I have the sinking feeling we're doomed."

"No need to be a prophet of gloom," Agatha chided. "We're not even halfway to the finish. Perhaps something even worse will happen to the *Queen*."

"Probably wishful thinking," Lily said drolly.

"What do you mean?" Jack queried. "Something worse has already happened to the *Queen*. She hasn't got Hoyt for a captain, and that's a huge disadvantage in itself," he claimed. "Hoyt knows how to steer a true course, and coax the best out of his men. Those two factors alone are enough to give any ship he commands a considerable edge." He shoved back from the table. "Having said my piece, I'd better get up to the pilothouse in case I can be of any help to him."

When he had gone, Lily said sheepishly, "If we have any doubts about winning, we'd better not voice them around Captain Jack."

Agatha looked dubious. "I know Hoyt's among the best, but I hope Jack's not expecting miracles from him."

During the next hour, the *Lily Belle* struggled to prevent the *Queen* from gaining an even larger lead.

Lily had purchased a newspaper from the newsstand, and was perusing an advertisement for Caramel Cereal, a beverage claimed by the Battle Creek Sanitarium Health Food Company to be a healthy alternative to coffee and tea, when Agatha let out a loud whoop.

"Look, my dear!" she insisted, shoving the binoculars into Lily's hands. "Something dreadful must have happened aboard the *Queen*. Her smoke is down to a wisp and in no time, we'll be by her."

Lily stared through the glasses. Sure enough, the *Queen* had obviously suffered a tremendous loss of power. Lily lowered the binoculars, grinning broadly, as she tapped her fist on the table. "By golly, we might just beat her to port, after all. I'm going out on deck to take a better look."

She was staring at the *Queen*, gloating over the swift manner in which the *Lily Belle* was about to take command of the lead, when Pettish appeared by her side.

"What do you suppose is going on over there?" he asked.

"I don't know what to think, but strictly off the record, I hope it's serious."

Pettish pocketed his pen. Arching his brow wickedly, he admitted, "I'm hoping they blew a boiler. That would keep them at quite a disadvantage from here on in."

Lily grinned conspiratorially. "That it would, but I suppose we shouldn't get our hopes up. The last line won't be written for—" she consulted the watch on her pendant, "another hour at least."

Pettish pulled out his own watch, then made verbal and written notes. "Four twenty-three P.M., the *Lily Belle* regains the lead." Capping his pen, he fictitiously added, "For the last time."

"I hope it's so," said Lily. Feeling the chill of the damp air, she traded the brisk, clean breeze of the deck for the warmth of the lounge, where Captain Jack's pipe was wreathing her table in a delicious vanilla haze. For twenty

120

minutes, the room buzzed with optimism as the *Huron Queen* dropped farther and farther behind.

Later, Jack was the first to notice the competitor creeping up on the *Lily Belle* once more, and for twenty minutes, she gradually improved her position until approximately a quarter mile back. The finish line lay a little over seven miles off.

Whether afraid of again being overtaken, or heeding some sixth sense, Jack excused himself to go below to the engine room. Pettish followed in his wake, but when Jack ignored him, descending the stairs which were off limits to the special crew members, the news editor made straight for Lily and Agatha.

"Did Wilson say something was wrong? Why did he go below?"

Lily rose from the table. "He didn't say. You're on your own now, Mr. Pettish. I'm going to the pilothouse. Unfortunately for you, only authorized personnel are allowed there."

In the glass chamber of Hoyt's realm, Lily could have cut the tension with a knife. Thad, the navigator of the *Lily Belle*, was at the port window with binoculars tracking the progress of the competition, while Hoyt manned the helm, his wheelsman standing close by.

Hoyt's jaw was working harder than usual, and Lily could almost hear his teeth grinding. She was tempted to inject levity into the solemn scene by quipping that her crew was loafing again, as usual, but she dared not, lest she be bodily removed from their presence.

Joining Thad at the window, she borrowed the glasses. How helpless she felt, watching the *Queen* coming down on them with the sureness of a boulder starting downhill. Up ahead, in the distance, were several smaller craft. Likely two of these were the stakeboats, but from this great a distance, Lily couldn't pick out their distinguishing markings. The dull droning of the engines was punctuated by Jack's gravelly voice as he burst into the pilothouse.

"Captain, with permission, I'm taking Thad below. I've got a steam inlet valve slow in closing, and he's the only man small enough to ride the rod till we cross the line."

"Permission granted," Hoyt clipped without any sign of the sluggishness that usually plagued his speech. "Is the *Queen* still closing on us?" he asked Lily.

"I'm afraid so, Captain."

"Can you pick out the stakeboats yet?"

She switched her line of vision to the vessels ahead. Government patrol boats flying white flags with the black letter P were busy keeping boatloads of curious spectators at a safe distance from the two tugs marking the end of the race. "I'd estimate we're still two miles off the finish line, Captain, and from strictly an amateur navigator's point of view, you appear to be exactly on course."

"Thank you," said the captain.

She looked again at the *Queen*. The opposition was even nearer to catching up, trailing by only a few lengths now, but the *Lily Belle* seemed to be picking up a little steam, her engines vibrating a tad faster. Thad's presence below must be making a difference, Lily concluded, but would it be enough?

Pilothouse conversation gave way to the humming of the engines while Lily, Hoyt, and the wheelsman concentrated on the *Lily Belle's* progress toward the finish line.

A mile from the end of the race, the stakeboats were now easily identifiable without glasses. To either side of the finish line, small steamers passed back and forth, their passengers eager to witness first hand the end of the greatest race Lake Michigan had ever seen.

With a half mile to go, the *Lily Belle's* lead had narrowed to about two hundred yards.

Jack came through the door. Passing Hoyt and the wheelsman to stand by Lily, he claimed determinedly, "We're gonna take this race."

Lily kept her silence, chewing the inside of her lip as the *Queen* continued to creep up.

A quarter mile from the finish. The *Lily Belle* possessed but a three-length advantage.

For the next few critical seconds, she somehow managed to hold onto it as she crossed the finish line!

Tugs, steamers, fishing boats, and even a sailing yacht let loose with a loud chorus of whistle blasts.

"We've done it!" Jack claimed triumphantly.

"It's not official," Hoyt reminded him.

All eyes were on the judges' boat. Moments later, three kites, the signal for the *Lily Belle's* victory, rose in gray skies.

Jack let out the loudest whoop Lily had ever heard. "Congratulations, Captain!" He slapped his victorious friend on the shoulder.

Though Hoyt kept his silence as he concentrated on slowing down the vessel and bringing her around, a wide grin registered his satisfaction.

Turning to Lily, Jack dropped his cane and cradled her face with his calloused hands, placing a smacking kiss on her forehead. "Congratulations, Mrs. Haynes. I hope you're prepared for one whale of a celebration, because I know a crew that deserves a party."

"One 'whale of a celebration' coming up!" Lily promised.

As a boatload of spectators passed the victorious steamer, passengers hung over the rail, waving and shouting jubilantly.

Bringing the *Lily Belle* around, Hoyt hailed the *Queen* with a blast of his whistle, but his salute went unanswered.

When the *Lily Belle* neared the channel in preparation for docking, Lily could hardly believe the mass of people jamming the sandy beaches along either side. The Black River was choked with traffic nearly as thick as that in Chicago. At her pier, a crowd awaited the ship's arrival, and carriages and hacks stood at the ready along Water Street to bear her crew's officers to the big house on the hill.

It seemed the whole town had turned out to welcome home the champion. Though a chant went up demanding the appearance of the captain, Hoyt could not be persuaded to show himself until his crewmen had completed their docking routines. When they assembled with him on the main deck, a deafening roar filled the air.

Ignoring his protestations, his men lifted him onto their shoulders and followed Lily, Agatha, and Jack down the gangplank to the elegant Cunningham coach that had been draped with blue and white crepe for the occasion. When the four of them had situated themselves inside, a jubilant parade, consisting of the crew and celebrating townsfolk and led by the beautiful plumed matched grays that drew Hoyt's carriage, marched up the hill.

Sitting on the front seat beside Hoyt, Lily waved and threw kisses to the supporters who lined the streets. Giving a backward glance, she fretted to Hoyt through her firmly fixed smile. "There must be a thousand or more people following us. I planned enough food for only our regular and special crew members and their families."

Though Hoyt leaned toward her and used his command voice to answer, Lily could just hear him above the din of a cheer that had erupted. "Don't worry. The others won't impose."

Horses prancing, they continued into the semi-circular drive at the corner of Erie and St. Joseph. The driver brought the coach to a stop and Hoyt lifted Lily from the step, regretting the move when he realized she had begun to increase, though slightly, with child, and he should not have squeezed her in the waist.

Lily landed lightly on her feet none the worse for Hoyt's assistance, and while Jack and Agatha climbed out of the back seat, she led Hoyt by the hand onto the veranda to face the throng of men arriving in her front yard. Putting hands up for silence, she waited for an opportunity to speak, amazed at the expedient manner in which a polite hush spread over her enthusiastic audience.

Before her were many faces she recognized: Thad, Hoyt's navigator, and Fairfield, the purser; stewards and stewardesses, cooks and waiters. Behind the above-decks crew were those who had kept the furnaces burning hot enough to steam to victory, the seldom-seen faces of engineers and coal passers, stokers and firemen, and their wives and children. Beyond them, as Hoyt had assured her, the villagers hung back.

She thought of what she had said when she had faced her crewmen this morning, and tried to think of the right words to say now, for she hadn't planned a victory speech. Her heart nearly rose to her throat as she began to speak.

"I want you to know how proud I am of each and every one who had a hand in achieving our victory today. I thank you," she paused to turn to Hoyt, "and your captain." An extemporaneous "Bravo, Captain Curtiss" briefly erupted. She continued her speech in the ensuing silence. "Now that we've tasted victory, it's time to celebrate this occasion

125

properly and taste the wonderful dinner that's waiting for you under the tent!" More cheers filled the air.

Her hand on Hoyt's arm, Lily had taken the first step leading off the porch when a strange silence began to fall over the gathering, and heads turned toward Erie Street. The townsfolk drew aside, revealing the reason for the sudden quiet.

Stepping forth with a swagger was Alick Haynes, accompanied by his chief engineer, Max Taggart.

CHAPTER

10

Lily continued her descent from the porch with Hoyt, taking comfort in the company of Jack and Agatha.

From his lofty height, Alick Haynes spared looks for no one but Lily, whom he fixed with an icy stare. Speaking with the diction of an orator, he declared for all to hear, "Ten thousand dollars says the *Huron Queen* will beat the *Lily Belle* in a rematch."

Hands on hips, Lily took a tiny step forward, head tipped back to meet Alick's frigid gaze with a look that blazed blue smoke. "The *Lily Belle* could beat—"

Jack stepped forth, his tug at Lily's elbow causing her to back off. Facing Alick with a mean scowl, he demanded, "What do you mean, coming up here where you're not welcome and issuing such a challenge?"

Lily quickly followed up. "Yes, what do you mean?"

Jack continued. "You've had your chance to prove yourself, Haynes. Now I've got but two things left to say about the race, so you'd better hear me, and hear me well. It was fair, and it was *final*!"

Alick turned to Lily for confirmation, and though she wasn't completely apprised of the reasons for Jack's position, she trusted him. "Did you hear that, Mr. Haynes? Final! Now if you'll take your leave, my guests and I will carry on with our victory celebration."

While Jack and Lily firmly faced Alick, Hoyt took Max aside. "You ran a fine race, Taggart." He offered a hand to the engineer, whom he had known and respected for many years.

Taggart shook readily. "Thanks, Cap'n. I believe we'd

a' caught ya' if it hadn't a' been for my bypass. I routed high pressure steam into the low pressure receiver. Got back pressure 'n had t' make changes."

"We made some mistakes, too," Hoyt admitted. Shaking once again, he added, "See you on the lake, Taggart."

The brawny engineer joined Alick. They turned down the driveway, eyes to the ground as whispered comments rippled through the onlookers. From somewhere amidst the throng, Thad made his way to the edge of the crowd, and as Alick and Max passed him, he showed his pithiness by shouting, "Three cheers for our worthy competitor, the *Huron Queen!*"

With ever increasing volume, the crowd joined in three rounds of "Hip, hip, hooray!"

Though they never turned back, Alick acknowledged the recognition by a wave of his hand; Max, by lifting his cap from his head.

Lily's party pleased her crew enormously. Though she hadn't planned it, the galley crew of her ship pitched in to assist in serving the fishboil from the huge cauldrons Ridgley and Margaret had simmered with, among other tasty ingredients, trout, potatoes, onions, bay leaves, parsley, and thyme.

A long buffet table offered sweet and tender corn on the cob, succulent summer squash, delectable blueberry bread, and for dessert, an array of choices from simple peaches and cream to dainty blueberry tarts, to an exquisite three-layer cake, decoratively piped by Ridgley's skilled hand with colored frosting depicting the shield of the *Lily Belle*.

While the adults lingered over dessert, children were excused to pursue their favorite summertime activities, and Lily was thankful that some mothers had thought to have their children bring along the essentials.

Boys formed up teams for a ball game in the back yard while girls skipped over hopscotch squares on the front sidewalk or challenged one another in jump rope competitions. By sunset, adults had had their fill of racing conversation, children had worked off some of their abundant energy, and families gathered again to take their leave.

From the fussy preparations to the hectic rush of serving over three hundred guests, and the more relaxed pace of cleaning up, Lily had noticed a pleasant and helpful rapport between Margaret and Ridgley, and despite the rather stuffy demeanor of the butler, she suspected perhaps more was developing between the couple than the shared responsibility for bringing off a successful party.

In British households, such as the one in which Ridgley had likely served before coming to America to work in Jack's home, fraternization among domestics would have been considered taboo, but in the states, such was not the case. Perhaps Ridgley had been able to overcome the strict standard carried over from his home country, and had allowed himself to consider alternatives to bachelorhood. A companionship between the butler and maid could be quite convenient, Lily thought, considering the alliance which had developed between their employers.

In the weeks that followed, the big race was the talk of Lake Michigan. Business was better than ever for the *Lily Belle*, but the improvement came about not so much due to her winning, as in response to the new interest post-race publicity had stirred up for the *Huron Queen* on her home waters.

According to Jack, Alick Haynes had only chartered the

ship through the beginning of August, and though he continued to run on the same schedule as the *Lily Belle* for the week following the race, the owners of the Detroit & Cleveland Line were flooded with requests to run the *Huron Queen* again between Detroit and Mackinac Island, and she was returned to her old route where she was making more profit than ever.

With the removal of the *Queen* from Lake Michigan waters, the *Lily Belle* sailed full each time out, booking as many passengers as she was certified to carry, and loading every last square inch of her freight deck. By the last week of August, she had made substantial progress in paying for herself, showing considerable profit for the season above and beyond her running expenses.

During the same week, Lily received a letter from Victoria Bartlett, her friend on Mackinac Island, saying she had adjusted well to her new role as mother of a baby girl, and was looking forward to entertaining friends. She invited Lily to visit her on the island, explaining that she and her husband, Rand Bartlett, manager of Grand Hotel, would remain on the island until early October, at which time they would return to their Detroit residence.

The correspondence reminded Lily of a promise she had made earlier in the season to Agatha, and spawned an idea she decided to sound out with reliable Sweetwater Steamship associates. She asked Hoyt, Jack, Agatha, and her purser, Mr. Fairfield, to meet with her in her office on the return of the *Lily Belle* from Milwaukee the following afternoon.

They faced each other across the oak pedestal table which Margaret had set with coffee, tea, and Caramel Cereal for Lily, along with a trayful of Ridgley's excellent cheese wafers. With Purser Fairfield's records before her, Lily proposed her plan.

"Now that our first season is nearly over, I thought it would be nice to reward the crew of the *Lily Belle* for their hard work in making her successful. I'd like to take the entire Sweetwater Steamship family to Mackinac Island for Labor Day weekend. We could depart South Haven on Saturday morning and leave from the island early Monday. Accommodations and meals would be provided by the line for all crew members and their families, but I'm not about to hire on extras to run the ship, so everyone would have to man his or her post while in transit."

Agatha clapped her hands. "Why, I think that's an excellent idea, Lily. I've thought from the start, you should take the *Lily Belle* to the island."

"Could I see the purser's records?" Jack asked.

Lily passed him the ledger she had been studying. "You've impressed on me how important it is to treat my employees well. I see no reason why they shouldn't be entitled to some benefit from the profits they helped earn."

Purser Fairfield, a forty-year-old gentleman with gold-rimmed glasses and a center part dividing his thinning brown hair, leaned forward over the pair of neatly folded hands he had set on the table. "With all respect, Mrs. Haynes, the expense of such an excursion is quite considerable."

"I realize that," Lily assured him, "but the good morale of my employees is beyond price. Perhaps more than anyone, you yourself deserve some reward for service rendered. If not for your discovery of Alick's fraudulent practices last May, we would not be sitting here today." Handing him a ledger sheet, she said, "I've already worked up this proposed budget. Please tell me if I've left anything out."

131

While Jack and Purser Fairfield perused figures, Lily turned to Hoyt, who was seated beside her. "You're being your usual quiet self, Captain Curtiss. Tell me, would such a trip meet with your favor, or are the difficulties of navigating the straits a challenge a Lake Michigan man would rather decline?"

Hoyt understood immediately Lily's strategy to gain unanimous support, and though she had put him in a corner, forcing him to agree or suffer serious damage to his ego, he admired her ingenuity. "Thad has charted courses through the straits many times. I'm favorable," he declared, successfully routing himself out of the dilemma.

Lily's impish smile told him she admired his verbal maneuverings through treacherous channels.

Jack slapped shut the purser's record book. "I say we do it. Thad deserves a change of routine, not to mention the reward for having ridden out the big race on a rising and falling valve rod. He gave us the edge we needed to stay ahead and win, you know."

Though Lily hadn't known, she was even more pleased realizing Thad, along with the rest of the crew, would soon be treated to a stay at one of the finest resort islands in the Midwest.

Though neither Jack nor Agatha would have required their servants on the three day trip, Lily suggested Margaret and Ridgley be included. Margaret had visited Mackinac Island three summers ago, but Ridgley would be seeing it for the first time, and unbeknownst to either of them, they would be given ample time to explore the emerald wonderland.

From her seamstress, Lily commissioned an adorable dress for her friend's baby daughter—all silk and lace and ribbons with a smocked yoke, and a darling bonnet to match. Agatha, too, chose a gift for Victoria, whom she had come to know and respect during the summer of '95—an engraved silver cup.

In the days before departure, Jack made arrangements for a special dinner on Saturday night to be held aboard the *Lily Belle*. Through Reverend Gillis, his longtime friend now serving as pastor on Mackinac Island, a group of capable church women would, in return for a charitable contribution, serve a delicious family style meal, thus allowing the galley and dining room staffs of the steamer a respite from their duties during the holiday weekend.

In the dark of morning on the fourth of September, Lily and Agatha descended the hill from Erie Street to join others of the Sweetwater Steamship Line on the *Lily Belle*. Jack had spent the night on board with Hoyt, seeing that all provisions for the three day trip were accounted for.

Stewards and stewardesses, allowed to dress in civilian attire rather than their starched white uniforms, were in buoyant spirits knowing they would be performing their services not for paying passengers, but for their own families, and those of other crew members.

With the first light of dawn, the *Lily Belle* emerged onto a calm lake from South Haven's channel, sounding her farewell blast as she cleared the light on the south pierhead, pointing northward on the route that would end fifteen hours and two hundred eighty miles later at the sparkling gem of the Straits of Mackinac. Appropriate for the occasion, Lily brought along the counted cross stitch piece depicting Mackinac Island which she had worked on sporadically since last spring, and took up residence at the table she and Agatha had so often occupied in the main lounge. Perhaps now, with the shipping season nearly over, she would make some significant progress on her needlework.

By the time the *Lily Belle* entered the harbor at Mackinac Island, a dusky shroud had begun to settle over her curving shoreline and the bluffs on either side of the bay. Even so, from the promenade deck Lily could make out the impressive white façade of Grand Hotel. The grand lady dominated the hillside from which she reigned over lesser hostelries and tourist homes, eateries and fudge shops, Indian bazaars and trinket vendors, all tightly jammed together on Main Street and Market Street below. To the east, Lily took in the familiar sight of the gently rising white limestone wall leading to Fort Mackinac, and the officers' quarters and guardhouse situated behind.

As the *Lily Belle* made fast at the pier, her owner looked forward to tomorrow morning when she would renew her acquaintance with Victoria, and meet the new addition to the Bartlett household, tiny Rosalind. The thought of seeing them made Lily anxious to go ashore.

She would walk again on the magnificent veranda of Grand Hotel from which the view of the straits, with Round Island and its lighthouse and the constant parade of steamers passing between Lakes Michigan and Huron, was unequaled. But was she ready for the memories it would evoke of Parker and their times together here?

A thought stole into her mind like a message from her Maker: You can let go of the sadness in your past, make room for new joy, and still respect Parker's place in your heart. A peaceful feeling came over her, and she believed that over time, she would lay to rest old ghosts.

Congenial voices wafted to her from the decks below. Some of the boiler room boys were disembarking now to begin their celebrations of the long holiday weekend. Jack was following behind. He had told Agatha this afternoon that he would not be spending the evening with her, explaining that he wanted to make sure the young fellows didn't get rowdy in town and give the ship a bad name. The plan came as no great disappointment to Agatha since he had been by her side during almost the entire fifteen-hour trip.

The weather this night was balmy, too perfect to waste, and Lily felt a little too excited to retire to her cabin just yet, but she supposed she should join Agatha there and turn in early.

She had started toward the parlor deluxe when she met up with Hoyt in the passageway. She hadn't seen much of him on this cruise, nor had she expected to, the route being out of the ordinary.

"Going ashore?" she asked, for he had traded his uniform for a natty pair of white trousers with waist pleats, a brass buttoned navy blue blazer with matching vest and white shirt beneath, and a jaunty blue cap sporting heavy brass cord over the visor. The wholesome scent of cedar tinged the air, and she realized he must have stored his coat with chips of this fragrant wood in the pockets.

"Need to stretch my legs. Walk with me?" He knew he shouldn't have asked. She probably needed her rest. Most women in her condition seemed to require an abundance of it, but he had heard walking was considered good exercise for one who is *enceinte*. Besides, he had barely seen a glimpse of her since the decision to take the trip a week ago, and he just plain missed her bubbly spirit.

Tucking her hand in his elbow, she felt a new surge of energy, and nearly led him down the deck toward the gangplank. "A walk is just what I need. I'm so glad you asked, Captain Curtiss. Which direction have you in mind?"

He shrugged. "You decide."

As they came off the dock, Lily turned east and paused in front of Hulbert's store. The nearly darkened window displayed an attractive blue dress of grass linen. Its bodice was shirred, with the front of white silk embroidery and a striking white lace cravat tied in a large bow. The sleeves were styled in the newest Paris fashion, puffed at the shoulders, then fitted to the arm, ending in frills of lace at the wrists.

The skirt was pleated down the front, with a full, gathered back. A collar and belt of pale blue taffeta complemented the elegant design, which was set off by a black straw hat slightly rolled at one edge, and trimmed with straw loops and thick, curled ostrich feathers.

Hoyt thought how attractive the blue gown would look on Lily, bringing out the sapphire in her eyes.

Having thoroughly appraised the fashion, Lily gave a thoughtful laugh and continued on. "In the past, I would have purchased such a frock," she explained, "but I'll be wearing black for quite awhile. Besides, I have my increasing waistline to consider. At least my friend, Victoria, has all that behind her. Knowing Tory, she's probably already slender as ever and back in her regular dresses . . . I can't wait to see her again. Did I ever tell you how we met?"

Hoyt loved hearing Lily rattle on. She seemed effervescent tonight, and her ability to furnish the bulk of the conversation pleased him. She needed little encouragement to keep her going, and he willingly supplied the few appropriate words. "How did you meet her?"

Lily drew a long breath, and Hoyt figured it was enough wind to keep her in full sail until they had reached the foot of the hill by Fort Mackinac, two blocks down.

"It was two summers ago," she began. "Margaret couldn't come with Auntie to the island because her mother had taken ill back in Ireland, and Auntie had sent her home. I, on the other hand, had gotten myself into a peck of trouble by trying to elope with the wrong kind of man, as my mother called him. My gentleman friend and I were caught before we had even slipped out of the house. That's when Mother decided she had had her fill of my imprudent behavior and banished me from Newport to Mackinac to serve as Auntie's companion. Mother figured I was safe here, under Agatha's eagle eye, and she was right. I could barely stir from my bedroom to the washroom without her knowing.

"I had been here about a week when Tory came to Grand Hotel. The establishment owed her papa money. Thanks to Auntie and me, we matched her up with the hotel manager, netting her not only the overdue funds, but a husband, besides!" She stopped to look up at Hoyt who wore a rather bemused expression. "So let that be a lesson to you," she warned playfully. "Auntie and I are liable to pair you off, and in no time, some young miss will have you hook, line, and sinker!"

Hoyt gave a hearty laugh, to which Lily responded with her exaggerated frown.

"I'm warning you, unmarried people aren't safe around Auntie and me. Take your friend, Captain Jack. Why, she's nearly got him wrapped around the silver handle of her mahogany cane!"

"I've noticed," Hoyt admitted. Though his friend was most discreet in matters of the heart, he had long ago confided his singular affection for Agatha Atwood.

Lily leaned close and half whispered, "Auntie and I even have secret plans to pair off Ridgley and Margaret on this very trip," she revealed.

"Quite a challenge," Hoyt said meaningfully.

They had come to the end of the block, and crossed the street to return on the opposite side. In those few moments, quiet enough to hear the calls of bats soaring over the fort gardens, Lily became thoughtful.

"You know, we've faced a lot of challenges since I began managing the *Lily Belle*. We solved the problems Alick broke over our bows, and we outran him and the *Huron Queen*, but—" she gazed down at her abdomen, "I believe I'm going to face my biggest challenge about five months from now." Looking up at Hoyt, she admitted with a tenuous smile, "And I'm a little scared."

Hoyt quietly assured her, "You don't have to face it alone."

In the dim light, he could see the merry sparkle gradually returning to her eyes. "I know. Why, Agatha is so looking forward to my first child. It will be almost like a great grandchild to her, since she's always considered me more of a granddaughter."

Hoyt paused, turning her to face him. "I meant me," he quietly declared. "I'll b . . . be there, if you want."

Unsure how to answer, Lily simply gazed into the kind, broad face of the man who had already given her support beyond reason.

In the rare moment when Lily's tongue seemed out of steam, Hoyt gave voice to thoughts he had kept locked in his heart for weeks, praying the words wouldn't snag on shoals of emotion. "I thought highly of Parker. His child deserves a father . . . when you're done mourning. I could be a good one. When the youngster is old enough to understand . . . I'd explain what a fine man Parker was." From the look on Lily's face, he could tell she was taken aback by his outspokenness. Offering his arm, he suggested, "Think on it awhile."

Had Lily been able to speak, her thoughts would have spilled forth in a torrent of questions. Though Hoyt had cared deeply for Parker, exactly how did he feel about her? Did he love her? In an era that placed great importance on the responsibility of women to rear children, he seemed anxious about the baby having no father. Why was he so concerned about Parker's child?

This seemed like such an obtuse way of proposing marriage. For how long after she was done mourning would he wait for an answer?

As she walked with him toward the dock, she gathered her thoughts. Hoyt was a Lake Michigan man. He was dedicated to his responsibilities as master of the *Lily Belle*. Could she again accept second place to a lake and her ship in her husband's heart? At one time, she had decided not, but now that she was more actively involved in running her vessel and steamship line, had her feelings changed?

Managing her life would be difficult enough with a new child added to the picture. How would she fare with a new husband, as well?

When they had again boarded the *Lily Belle*, she stood with Hoyt on the deck outside her stateroom, ready to share her conclusions.

"You know, Hoyt," she began, "this is the first time I've been on the island since I met Parker here two years ago, and I've learned something about myself in the hour or so since we tied up."

As he listened, she detected a slight wavering in his usually steady gaze. Hoping to put him at ease, she continued on the subject as delicately as she could. "I loved Parker, but even so, I've come a long way in recovering from his death. Regardless, the thought of another man in my life, and the prospect of raising the child Parker left

139

behind . . . I'm not sure I'm up to the responsibilities."

His mouth was open. He would say his piece, given time. She waited.

"That's why I g . . . gave you the gifts . . . the baby gifts." What a fine fix. Just when he needed his tongue most, it seemed not to know him. He tried again. "I thought you weren't looking forward to having the . . . baby and maybe they'd help put you in a . . . better frame of mind."

Lily recalled how distraught she was soon after learning of her pregnancy. It had added to her concern over managing the *Lily Belle*, and she had confided her worries in Hoyt. She wondered whether he had been planning his proposal all along.

"I wasn't trying to . . . buy your affection," he said, as if in answer to her unspoken question.

"No. Of course not," she reassured. Her eyes settled on the half-visible silvery orb above, and she tried to lighten the mood. "You know, Hoyt, I'm not sure what it is about this part of the lakes, but I think the moon spills some kind of magic dust over this one little island, and anyone who walks here might kick it up, and become vulnerable to affairs of the heart. Do you suppose, on our short little walk, you got moondust on your shoes?"

He gazed at the lovely woman before him, the way her pale blond hair waved softly back from her pretty, blushed cheeks, how her dainty nose curved up at the very end, like a child's would, giving her a look of innocence. But those sapphire eyes spoke more than even her quick tongue. In them, he had seen first a grieving widow, then a determined one who wasn't even afraid of Alick Haynes. They had let him know when she needed his support, and when she wanted to be independent. Now, they were saying even more than her words, that she was confused.

140

He could appreciate her convenient metaphor, but he was determined now to master his tongue well enough to speak clearly of the emotions that were rising within him.

CHAPTER
11

"Moondust or no, I love you, Lily, and I'm willing to wait for you. As long as it takes."

Hoyt's admission set Lily's heart—and mind—in a whirl. Her heart said to love him back, while her mind threw up a red flag of caution.

He was a kind, considerate man—more considerate than Parker—but would he change his ways if they were wed, as Parker had?

She struggled to find the right words, and wondered if perhaps she was now getting an inkling of the problem Hoyt faced each time he meant to speak. She would not make the mistake she had after he had showered her with baby gifts, blurting out words she didn't mean, but she must say something soon. He was shifting his weight, looking as though he were about to bid her good night. She couldn't let him go unanswered.

"I'm glad you're willing to wait," she managed in a voice too frail to be her own. She cleared her throat and spoke up. "I mean, I'll be a long time in mourning. I'm glad you're a patient man." She fumbled with the watch on the gold chain about her neck, finding the light from the moon and stars just bright enough to read the time. "I'd best say good night. It's getting late. You'll come with me and Auntie and Jack tomorrow afternoon to meet Tory and her husband, won't you? They're sending a carriage from Grand Hotel to fetch us at one."

Hoyt's smooth, calm answer quelled her nerves like oil on water. "I'll plan on it. Until then." He touched his finger to the brim of his cap, then disappeared in the darkness, his heels clicking as he strode confidently toward the bow.

In the parlor deluxe, Agatha was sitting up in bed, propped against two plump goose down pillows while she read from a volume of Benjamin Franklin's quotations. She removed her pince-nez and laid the book aside when Lily entered.

"You look tired and a mite pale, niece. Are you feeling all right?"

Lily perched on the edge of Agatha's bed. "I'm not sure, Auntie—I mean, physically I'm fine. Emotionally, I'm not certain what to think."

"It's Hoyt, isn't it?"

"How did you guess?"

A knowing smile deepened the furrows about Agatha's mouth. "Process of elimination, forgive the double meaning. It had to be either Parker, or Hoyt. Only men can put that look on your face. Since you seem to have come to terms with Parker's death over these past several weeks, I assumed it must be Hoyt. He's mighty fond of you, isn't he?"

Lily nodded.

"I've known lots of fellows over the years, and I can assure you they don't come much better than Hoyt Curtiss. He's a fine, sensitive man. He'd do right by you and your child, Lily, but I suspect by the time you're done mourning, you won't need me telling you. You'll know that for yourself."

"But Auntie, he'll be on the water for months and months during the shipping season, year in, year out."

"So go with him."

Evidently not listening, Lily continued. "I found out about lake men when I married Parker, and I don't intend to make the same mistake twice. It's a lonely life."

Agatha tried again. "Don't you see it's different this time? You and Hoyt are both working very hard for the same thing, to make Sweetwater Steamship Line the best. You need him, he needs you. If you want, you can spend as much time aboard the *Lily Belle* as he does, and your child, too. There's many a family been raised aboard a steamer, and before that, sailing ships."

Lily went to the dresser and began taking down her hair, brushing it in front of the mirror. Her thoughts tumbled in confusion as she moved mechanically through her routine, unhooking bodice and skirt, unlacing hightop shoes, unbuttoning her combination garment, and slipping into her pink silk negligee. She was as confused as ever when she unwrapped the chocolate heart left on her pillow by the stewardess who had turned back her bed.

Agatha was still reading Franklin, and looked up from the book. "'Keep your eyes wide open before marriage, half-shut afterwards.'" She laid the volume aside.

Lily was still trying to puzzle out the Franklin quotation when Agatha said, "Lily, if you haven't plans for tomorrow morning, let's go shopping, then to luncheon at the Astor House."

"Shopping and luncheon would be fine, but Auntie, what does Franklin mean?"

"He means you're doing fine, Lily. You're taking a good look before remarrying. As for the rest, you'll have to decide for yourself. Good night, dear." She doused the light, and had commenced snoring when Lily finally decided to give up on interpreting the rest of the quotation.

She spent an hour or more pondering Hoyt's declaration of love, finally telling herself she wouldn't need to decide about Hoyt, or anyone, for several months. At last, she

144

drifted off to sleep.

The morning brought partly cloudy skies, and Lily wondered about the threat of rain as she and Agatha walked the short distance from the *Lily Belle* to Hulbert's, where she had admired the blue dress the evening before. Despite Lily's protestations, Agatha insisted on buying the dress for her to wear after the baby came, and for herself, purchased a new pair of navy kid gloves with four large pearl buttons at the wrist, and a fine matching silk lace hat trimmed with ribbon, rhinestone buckle, and a large spray of fine velvet and muslin roses and forget-me-nots.

For Jack, she purchased a new solid gold vest chain, black silk embroidered fancy dress suspenders, and a black four-in-hand silk tie.

"My. Anyone would think the two of you were planning to do the town," Lily commented. "I haven't seen either of you in such fancy furnishings."

"You never know!" Agatha answered cryptically.

She had the goods sent over to the *Lily Belle*, where the stewardess would deliver it to her cabin, then treated Lily to a luncheon at the Astor House, where fricassee of veal with green peas was the order of the day, served with chilled apple juice, chicken noodle soup, sliced tomatoes, boiled potatoes, and for dessert, wine-cured Stilton cheese. By half past twelve, they had returned to the ship to freshen up for the visit to Grand Hotel.

An elegant vis-à-vis pulled by a plumed team of prancing roans arrived at the dock promptly at one o'clock, the footman in his tail coat, gloves, and top hat jumping quickly down to see everyone aboard. Lily and Hoyt took the front seat, allowing them a breathtaking view of ultramarine water and hazy islands when the vehicle reached the top of Cadotte Avenue, the road that carried traffic from the water-front village to the famous hotel on the hill.

Passing by the row of tall, white columns that lined the west wing of the portico, the coach stopped beneath the *porte-cochère*, and Hoyt helped Lily to alight. On the landing of the wide, carpeted stairs, Victoria Bartlett awaited her guests, and Lily could see that her predictions had been correct. The new mother was indeed in fine form.

Her toilet no longer consisted of the conservative suit which had characterized her wardrobe two years ago. Instead, her willowy figure did justice to a cashmere gown in medium blue, its tight-fitting sleeves topped by double caps trimmed with black ruchings—a style direct from Paris, Lily was certain, for she had seen nearly an identical design recently on the women's page of the *Tribune*.

Victoria's thick, dark hair had been attractively styled to curl softly about her face, then was drawn loosely into a topknot rather than skinned back as before. She wore a bit of rouge and lip color now, too, which complemented nicely her fair complexion and dawn-gray eyes.

"How good to see you, my friend!" Victoria greeted, her arms open to receive Lily's hug.

The rhythm and timbre of Victoria's voice had mellowed a bit from its businesslike tone of two years ago, but Lily would have recognized it anywhere and was comforted in hearing it.

Lily stepped back, taking a long look at Victoria. "My, but you are looking too marvelous to be the mother of a six-week-old infant. I can hardly wait to see Rosalind!"

"And I can hardly wait to show her to you," Victoria admitted with a wide smile. Her eyes straying to Agatha, she extended her hand. "Mrs. Atwood, you're looking as young as ever." She bent down to kiss the diminutive

146

woman on her cheek.

"Mrs. Bartlett, my dear, you wear motherhood well," Agatha praised.

"You're so kind," she replied, and turned again to Lily. "You must introduce me to your friends."

"My pleasure. Captain Jack Wilson, Captain Hoyt Curtiss, Mrs. Rand Bartlett, the feminine half of the management team running this fine establishment."

Victoria welcomed the gentlemen with a handshake, then discounted Lily's compliment. "I've had less time than usual for hotel business these past six weeks. I can't quite get used to the idea of leaving Rosalind's care to her nanny, yet the poor woman probably wishes I'd get on with my responsibilities as social director and let her be, so she can do her job."

As they climbed the last set of stairs and passed through one of the triple front doors giving entrance to the vast lobby, Lily asked, "Will we see your popular husband this morning, or is he beset by too much work, now that other priorities have laid claim to your time?"

Victoria laughed, likely recalling the disappearing act that had characterized Rand Bartlett during their courting days. "Rand has assured me he will put in an appearance before you take your leave, though he will undoubtedly have to be reminded by his secretary to do so."

They crossed the lobby beneath a vaulted ceiling supported by a series of white columns, taking the elevator to the third floor. Walking the length of the wide, plushly carpeted corridor to the left, Victoria showed her guests into a an apartment that comprised the end of the west wing.

"I see your father's hand in the carved furnishings. He does such exquisite work," said Lily, pausing to admire a hand rubbed oak parlor chair bearing a rose medallion at center back.

"The parlor suite was a wedding gift from Papa," Victoria explained.

"And how is your papa doing?" Lily asked, crossing to the divan near the window where Hoyt joined her.

"Busier than ever."

"He probably misses you dearly," Agatha ventured, settling on the parlor chair while Jack took the rocker beside her.

Victoria perched on a burgundy plush sofa. "I think he did when I first left Grand Rapids, but lately, someone else has been much on his mind. You see, he's thinking of remarrying!" Victoria's gray eyes sparkled with a hint of blue when she revealed the news.

"Well glory be," Agatha responded. "I do like to hear of a widower who has found love once again." She cast a fond look in Jack's direction.

Jack cleared his throat. "Don't know your papa, but he has my respect. Takes bravery to become a married man." He met Agatha's gaze, his expression softening. "Course the right woman can put a powerful lot of bravery in a man's heart."

Lily struggled to keep giggles of delight in check as her aunt offered Jack a smile of approval. The elderly captain, seemingly discomfitted, made a bid for support. "Isn't that right, Hoyt?"

The younger man simply grinned, then charted his own course around the awkward topic. "I like your view, Mrs. Bartlett," he said, pointing with a nod to the window that wrapped around the northwest corner of the apartment. It offered a stunning view of crescent-shaped Haldimand Bay, busy with steamers, rowboats, and sloops, as well as Round Island and its lighthouse, and in the hazy distance, heavily wooded Bois Blanc Island. Shoreside, the gables, veranda, and scalloped shingling of the neighboring Newberry cottage presented visual delights.

"Thank you, Captain Curtiss. It's my husband's favorite window, with the exception of those in the cupola, which isn't fit for family living."

"Speaking of family," Lily interjected, "when will we get a peek at your precious new addition?"

"Rosalind should be awake now. Nanny promised to have her ready for company by half past the hour. I'll see how they're getting along."

A minute later, Victoria returned cradling a waking Rosalind in her arms, bringing her precious bundle directly to Lily. "You want to hold her, don't you?" Victoria asked.

"Silly question, Mama," Lily said fondly. Taking the child, Lily realized she had rarely held such a young baby, but Rosalind fit comfortably in her arms. The infant stretched and yawned, making little baby noises, then kicked her tiny legs beneath the smocked gown Lily had sent as a gift.

Rosalind's Dresden china complexion, whisper of dark hair on an otherwise bald head, and fringe of black lashes about eyes that were just learning to focus, stirred a yearning in Lily for the arrival of her own child. She spoke softly to the babe, lightly stroking her plump, round cheek, unsuccessfully coaxing her to smile.

"Such a perfect little baby," Lily murmured. Rosalind replied with a whimper that quickly escalated to a howl.

Victoria immediately relieved Lily of the unhappy child, laughing when her friend quipped, "Like I said, such a perfect little baby, with a pair of perfectly developed lungs."

Rosalind soon quieted, as if in preparation for the arrival of her father a minute later.

149

Rand Bartlett swept into the apartment, seemingly a man of unlimited energy, but all too limited time. In the two years since Lily had last seen him, his compact physique and dapper style hadn't deteriorated a jot, though his chestnut hair was receding a bit now that he was entering his late thirties. As before, he sported a thick, neatly trimmed mustache.

When introductions and handshakes had been accomplished all around, he eagerly joined his wife on the sofa, looking adoringly over her shoulder at his progeny. "So you've seen our little Rosalind. If I do say so myself, she's just about the prettiest thing on Mackinac right now. Don't you agree?" Allowing not a moment for response, he quickly added, "And speaking of beauty, the *Lily Belle* makes quite an impression sitting in the harbor. I've just come from town, and couldn't help admiring your namesake, Lily."

A "thank you" was on the tip of Lily's tongue, but the loquacious hotel manager was too fast-spoken. "I was wondering if you and those who made the voyage with you would be my guests at four o'clock tea tomorrow afternoon in the main parlor. Short notice, I know, but I'd like to do something special for you and your friends and crew."

"We'd love to come!" Lily responded enthusiastically.

Jack coughed. "You'll understand if the boiler room boys take a rain check. We can let the others know at dinner tonight."

"Wonderful!" Rand said, then consulted the watch in his vest pocket. "Well, I must get back to my work. If you'll give Tory an idea by noon tomorrow how many will attend, we'll be prepared to receive you at four."

Giving his wife a peck on the cheek, he said, "I'll see you at half past six for dinner, Tory." He departed as quickly as he had come.

Lily observed, "I thought marriage and family would have slowed him down just a little, but he's still shooting about like a comet, Tory." Lily resorted to the nickname she had given her friend within moments of their first meeting and which, despite Victoria's initial objections, had obviously survived intact.

"Rand has given up managing the hotels in Petoskey and Detroit so he can remain constantly on the island during the summer season," Victoria explained.

Lily gave a thought to wondering whether marriage and family would slow Hoyt down, or if they would all travel together, as Agatha had suggested.

Agatha recalled, "From the first, I knew Rand Bartlett was a man of good judgment—knows where his time is best spent. I was certain he'd do right by you if you gave him a chance." She referred to advice she had given Victoria two summers earlier during a romance which had seemed constantly in the throes of crisis.

"And I am ever grateful for the wisdom you offered. My marriage has truly been blessed with happiness." She beamed at her little one.

As if on cue, Rosalind began to fuss, and while Victoria tried in vain to appease her, Lily suggested, "I think it's time we all go. Rosalind has probably had enough company for one day."

"I do believe she's developed an appetite," Victoria admitted, seeing her guests to the door. Above her baby's hungry cry, she said, "Until tomorrow afternoon."

Though under normal conditions, the boiler room and engine room crewmen were not allowed above decks, on Saturday evening they were invited to a family-style dinner

151

with the ship's officers, a thank you gesture by Lily for their good service throughout the season. Because the number of dinner guests was more than double the seating capacity of the dining room, tables were also set up in the main lounge.

Lily was glad that Jack had maintained his friendship with Reverend Gillis, who had once served as chaplain to mariners in Chicago and Detroit, but had since taken the call to fill the pulpit in the island church. Many from Lily's dining room and kitchen crews had already expressed their happy anticipation of the special dinner that would free them from their nightly duties. At four o'clock, twenty women from Reverend Gillis's church arrived on board to begin setting tables and preparing the meal, and by six, the dining room and lounge doors were opened.

In sharp contrast to the gourmet offerings normally produced by Lily's chef and skillfully served by waiters to meet the individual tastes of passengers, the ladies served an equally delicious, but less formal meal from large platters of thick slabs of ham steak, huge casserole dishes of sugary yams baked with apples, and giant bowls of good old fashioned stewed corn and tomatoes.

Yeast rolls, apple bread, and banana bread accompanied the main course, and for dessert, the church women offered a selection of pies to appease even the most stalwart appetite. There were coconut cream and lemon meringue, lattice topped apple and Dutch apple, pecan and mincemeat, and with them, coffee brewed rich and strong.

Reverend Gillis and his wife attended the *Lily Belle* family dinner, allowing Jack to renew his acquaintance with the burly minister who, had he removed his clerical collar, looked as though he would fit comfortably in the *Lily Belle's* engine room.

After the evening meal the three couples adjourned to

152

the deck. The Gillises expressed thanks to Lily for being invited, and Reverend Gillis suggested, "A filling meal such as this requires a bit o' fresh air. Could my good wife and I convince you all to ride with us to the parsonage? We've a few new photographs o' the children and grandchildren since Jack last saw us. Besides, it seems too soon to end such a pleasurable evening, and with the season about over, I'm not likely to see Jack again til next year."

"I think that's a wonderful idea," said Agatha, making a minor adjustment to her new hat. With all the fuss she had made over her toilet before dinner, Lily sensed the old woman would enjoy getting out to show off her finery. Jack, too, had dressed unusually well, using the furnishings Agatha had chosen for him at Hulbert's.

"Why don't the four of you go," prompted Lily. Though she found the Gillises likable enough, she wasn't eager to pore over family pictures of a couple she barely knew. She would prefer, instead, a stroll alone with Hoyt.

Mrs. Gillis's chubby hand took hold of Lily's. "But we want you to come, too, dear." The plump, white-haired woman began leading Lily off the ship, explaining, "I've been crocheting all summer long, and have quite run out of room in our tiny quarters for all that my hands produce. I was planning to give you some items to take home to South Haven." Her voice dropped as she added, "I have lots of pretty baby things."

Seeing that she couldn't graciously refuse, Lily went along, with Hoyt, Agatha, Jack, and the Reverend following behind.

The evening air had cooled, and as they drove past the park lands in front of the fort, it gave up its dockside fishy odor in favor of the milder essence of new mown, dewy grass. Robins hidden among the leafy branches of oaks and

153

maples filled the air with their good night tune, and bats came out of hiding to soar in the darkening sky. Beside Lily, Hoyt was quiet as usual, but something about the curve of his mouth made her wonder what he was thinking.

The little white parsonage, with its salt-box style roof, faced Fort Street, and though Mrs. Gillis had said little during dinner, she chattered almost nervously as she showed her guests into the keeping room.

"Now you just come on in and feel at home," she was saying, when Lily noticed a large bouquet of white roses and baby's breath on a butler tray table, a nosegay of the same beside it, two white rose boutonnieres, and a small cake frosted in white that bore this message:

Congratulations, Agatha & Jack

CHAPTER
12

Jack read Lily's puzzled look. "Lily, Hoyt, would you do Agatha and me the favor of bearing witness to our marriage? The Reverend has kindly consented to perform the ceremony for us here, now."

Lily caught her breath. "You're getting married? This evening?"

Agatha slipped her arm through Jack's. "That's right, dearie. You'll forgive us if we don't stay on the *Lily Belle* tonight."

With a sly smile, Jack explained, "I've booked us into a suite at Grand Hotel under an assumed name so your friends wouldn't know about our wedding plans beforehand."

Lily hugged her aunt impulsively, then Jack. "This is so exciting!" she bubbled. "I'm so very, very happy for you both." She beamed. Turning to Hoyt, she asked accusingly, "How long have you known about this?"

He shrugged innocently, appearing on the verge of an explanation when Jack came to his rescue.

"I think he figured it out this afternoon when I ordered the flowers, but I never actually told him the plan." Patting Agatha's hand, he added, "I'd promised someone very special I wouldn't breathe a word ahead of time, not even to Ridgley or Margaret, just in case things didn't quite work out."

Handing Agatha her bouquet, Lily said, "Well, they *did* work out, so let's get on with the ceremony." She pinned the boutonnieres on Jack and Hoyt, and taking a moment to inhale the glorious rose fragrance of her nosegay, stood in place beside her aunt.

The large open hearth fireplace, its mantle trimmed with tall brass candlesticks and a spray of Queen Anne's lace, made a lovely backdrop for the ceremony. Mrs. Gillis's vanilla almond cake proved delicious beyond any Lily could remember, despite her lack of appetite from the large dinner, and the gracious hostess promised to write down the recipe for her.

After a root beer toast to the newlyweds, Agatha and Jack asked Lily and Hoyt to deliver their personal notes of explanation to Margaret and Ridgley, and before the reverend drove the honeymooning couple to Grand Hotel, Lily tied huge long white streamers and an old shoe to his rig.

Agatha protested heartily at this outward display of the recently sealed marriage, but Lily could see that despite the elderly woman's objections, she was tickled pink to be a bride again after a decade of widowhood.

When the bridal couple had departed, Mrs. Gillis insisted Lily choose some baby caps and booties from those she had crocheted throughout the summer. The generous woman had not exaggerated about her busy hands, for her dresser drawer was packed full to overflowing with garments for the newborn.

Lily thanked Mrs. Gillis profusely for all she had done, and set out with Hoyt to walk back to the *Lily Belle*. The night sky was filled with a brilliant display of stars, and from the purple heavens hung a three-quarter moon the shade of a ripe lemon. The moist air, hinting of the roses in Lily's bouquet, caressed her cheeks with a dewy softness.

Taking a deep breath, she exhaled slowly. "I'm glad the excitement is over for one day."

Hoyt smiled down at her. In the lamp light, he could see her eyes were still aglow with happiness, and from the look on her face, her mind was working overtime.

As they turned toward the docks and the ship came into view, Lily shared her thoughts with him. "As soon as we've told Ridgley and Margaret about the wedding, I'll post a sign in the main dining room, and another in the crew's dining room . . . and I think I'll send a steward up to Grand Hotel with a message for Rand and Tory telling how many to expect for tea tomorrow, and asking if they can provide a little something special to celebrate the occasion."

Hoyt chuckled. "You just said the excitement was over."

Lily laughed at herself. "I guess I was wrong. I couldn't sleep unless I had shared the news with the whole crew. They've been like a second family to Jack this summer."

On the *Lily Belle*, Ridgley and Margaret were sitting on the aft deck, talking quietly as they watched moonbeams dance on the rippling bay waters. Lily couldn't help wondering if a little Mackinac moondust was working its way into their pores.

Ridgley, with dignity befitting an Englishman, responded to the news of his master's marriage with an unemotional but sincere, "I shall have to congratulate him."

Margaret, on the other hand, had come from a long line of emotional Irish stock, and casting decorum aside, blurted out, "Shamrocks and leprechauns! That's about the best news since the potato famine came to an end in old Ireland!" She lifted her skirt and danced a little jig.

Ridgley sighed disapprovingly, his nose in the air.

"You stodgy old Englishman," Margaret accused. "I'll shake some sentiment out o' you yet. Just you wait," she threatened, earning a begrudging smile from the butler, and outright laughter from both Lily and Hoyt.

Though clouds had begun to move in over the straits on

157

Sunday, and the morning winds brought the chilly foreshadowing of fall temperatures, Lily enjoyed walking to church with Hoyt. Agatha and Jack arrived in an opera coach from Grand Hotel, and must have been much pleased with Reverend Gillis's sermon on friendship, which seemed tailormade to honor the special relationships both he and Agatha had cultivated with Jack, and paralleling nicely the joy to be found in a loving relationship with God.

Following a light lunch on the *Lily Belle*, the two couples hired a driver to take them on a tour about the island. Along the west shore, they came first to the shallow caverns on the shoreline called Devil's Kitchen. Though an Indian legend had been associated with the erosions, telling of the terrors of the giant *Wen-di-goes* and their custom of roasting and eating men there, William Meade's newly published guidebook stated the name arose from the habit of an old islander who had used the place for his cooking and shoe cobbling.

A short distance beyond the caves was Pontiac's Lookout, where the cliff would have provided Indians with an excellent view of their enemies' approaching canoes. Here, Lily could sense the vastness of the waters surrounding the island, feel the stiffness of the prevailing breeze, fill her lungs with its fresh scent cleansed by the lakes.

A few minutes' ride brought them next to Chimney Rock, a limestone formation jutting up amidst tall pines beside the roadway. Here, the driver turned around to take them in the opposite direction, passing through town on Main Street, and proceeding to the attractions lying east of the village.

At the edge of the East Bluff, a ledge well over a hundred feet above the water commanded a view of the lakes and nearby Round Island and Bois Blanc. In former years, the lookout had projected over the beach, but the overhang had broken off, landing below in rock fragments.

Much confusion, including five different tales, surrounded the origin of the name of this place, Robinson's Folly, but Lily had read that it likely had association with Captain Robertson, the Englishman who had served as fort commandant in the late 1700's. According to one account, the captain had built a little bower house on the edge of the cliff and it had been destroyed when the precipice crumbled. Other tales linked the captain with an Indian maiden, giving rise to jealousies that eventually culminated in death by falling from the cliff.

With four o'clock drawing near, the driver returned his passengers to the ship where Lily and Agatha refreshed themselves before their engagement at Grand Hotel. As their carriage drew beneath the *porte-cochère*, Lily was exceedingly pleased to see her crew members arriving in their Sunday best: stewards, stewardesses, waiters and cooks looking fit enough to meet the Queen of England in their twills and tweeds, top hats and boaters.

Inside the grand entrance, the main parlor had been specially decorated with vases of white carnations and roses tied with wide blue bows—the colors of the *Lily Belle*—the theme carried out on the refreshment table where a white damask cloth and blue runner had been spread.

At the grand piano, a skilled musician sent forth the counterpoint of Bach Invention Number Eight, while liveried attendants filled cups and glasses with tea and punch. In the air hung the faintest hint of fine furniture polish, and Lily was certain the beautifully turned balustrade of the grand staircase had never glowed more warmly.

Tempting the palate was an array of tiny sandwiches and pastries, the fanciest Lily had seen, arranged pleasingly on

159

trays. Finger sandwiches of chopped chicken liver, beef, and cream cheese had been cut from crustless bread into the shapes of triangles, circles, and diamonds. White frosted petits fours with dainty blue adornments had been laid out beside row upon row of little tea cookies baked in Lily's favorite flavors—butter, chocolate, coconut, pecan, maple, and shortbread.

At the very end of the table were two wrapped gifts with cards for Agatha and Jack, and beside them stood a huge layer cake mounded with fluffy pink frosting and adorned with the leaves of a rose geranium. Several pieces had been cut and set out on plates, and Lily sampled one, savoring the delicate blend of the airy, white cake and boiled frosting.

Rand and Victoria seemed like old hands in their roles as host and hostess, chatting as comfortably with ship's officers as with the boys from the boiler room, who much to Jack's surprise, had chosen to attend an affair he had mistakenly assumed would hold little attraction for them.

After twenty minutes of quiet music and polite conversation, Rand asked one of his attendants to open a bottle of the very finest champagne. Though Lily could appreciate the expensive vintage, she chose to drink punch instead, having been warned by Dr. Adams to avoid alcohol during pregnancy. She felt comfortable in her choice since Tory, whom she had known as a teetotaler from two summers before, was drinking the same beverage.

When Rand's guests had been served, he offered a toast. "To Agatha and Jack, may you live all your lives in happiness!"

After a chorus of "Here, here," had gone up, and the champagne had been downed, glasses were filled for another round and Jack returned the toast. "To the Bartletts, may your congeniality be long remembered and appreciated by your guests!"

"To the Bartletts" went up heartily around the room and the glasses were again emptied. Rand Bartlett nodded his appreciation, his face beaming with delight at the enjoyment of his guests.

Victoria brought him one of the gifts from the table and he called for silence. "For Mr. and Mrs. Wilson, a token in remembrance of their wedding night at Grand Hotel."

From the box that had been beautifully wrapped in paper printed with the trademark of Grand Hotel, Agatha and Jack removed a silver candy dish engraved with the façade of the establishment.

A nod from Hoyt sent Thad to the table to claim the other gift and a hush fell over the gathering. In the same steady voice with which the pithy navigator had saluted Alick following the race, he presented the box to the newlyweds. "The crew of the *Lily Belle* wishes you many sweet moments of happiness."

Beneath the gold foil cover, Agatha revealed a large slab of vanilla pecan fudge on which had been written in chocolate, "Agatha and Jack, September 4, 1897."

One look at the fudge was almost enough to give Lily a stomach ache, remembering the five pounds of it Hoyt had given her following Parker's death. After nearly three months of eating a small portion every day, she had vowed she would never put another piece of the confection in her mouth, so when the box was sent around with a small silver knife for the guests to help themselves, she had no trouble passing it up.

When the tea ended at five o'clock, Lily thanked her good friends profusely for their graciousness and hospitality.

Outdoors, the late afternoon had turned sunny, and she and Hoyt decided to take advantage of the bright skies, walking rather than riding down the hill to the dock. The evening meal on the *Lily Belle* was both informal and light because of the abundant, rich offerings consumed at the tea. Jack and Hoyt spent their after supper hours preparing for the early morning departure while Lily and Agatha, with Margaret's assistance, settled the newlywed couple into a cabin of their own.

Skies were still black when the *Lily Belle* cleared the harbor the following morning. Her fifteen hour homeward bound voyage over calm waters seemed conducive to introspection, and Lily wondered how she could say good bye to Hoyt now that the passenger shipping season had come to an end. A feeling of melancholy came over her when she realized every waking moment since the ninth of July had been filled with responsibilities for the *Lily Belle*, and Captain Hoyt Curtiss had come to mean much more to her than just the master of her ship. Soon, he and a skeleton crew would depart South Haven for the last time, taking the *Lily Belle* to Manitowoc, Wisconsin for the winter where she would be refurbished for next year, and Hoyt would return to his Kewaunee home until spring.

Over those long, winter months, her life would change drastically. She would increase with child until sometime in February, when the miracle of birth would promote her to the much approved and admired status of motherhood. Though Hoyt's baby gifts had prepared her physical world for the coming child, emotionally Lily felt at a loss to deal with the promise of raising Parker's offspring.

Most certainly it would be a boy, which she would have no idea how to raise having spent no time at all around small boys. With her luck, he would probably also look exactly like his father! How she knew this, she could not say, except to think that in its present state, her mind was working rather perversely.

She thought of Hoyt's promise that she would not have to go through the blessed event alone, and that he loved her and would wait for her until she was past the mourning period. She also thought of her tenure as Parker's wife and knew she was not ready to think of Hoyt as a permanent part of her future.

No matter from which angle Lily looked at her situation, a long separation from Hoyt was inevitable. Attempting to take the positive approach, she told herself a little distance now might help her put her feelings for the captain into perspective, but she was little consoled by the thought.

As the *Lily Belle* neared South Haven, a knock sounded on Lily's cabin door. She opened it to Thad, who stood cap in hand in the narrow passageway.

"Sorry to disturb you, Mrs. Haynes, but could you please come to the main lounge? Some folks there would like to see you."

She followed him there immediately, half wondering why she had been called out, half sensing that she shouldn't ask questions. The assemblage waiting for her was impressive, filling the room to overflowing, and though she saw no coal passers or wheelsmen among the familiar faces, she wondered just who was running the ship. Certainly not Hoyt, around whom the gathering had centered, and to whom Lily was ushered by Thad.

Somehow, a large beribboned box materialized in the navigator's hands, and he cleared his throat to speak. "On behalf of your captain and all of your crew, I would like to thank you for taking us and our families to Mackinac Island."

More words of thanks came from those around her, and when a hush had again fallen, Thad continued. "This gift is our small way of saying thanks for a good season. We couldn't work for anyone finer than you, Mrs. Haynes!"

Applause went up, and Thad handed her the parcel which had that all too familiar look of a fudge shop's gold foil. She gazed down at the weighty package, consciously reminding herself to be grateful. "I'm really quite over-whelmed by your thoughtfulness," she said with complete honesty.

From a few onlookers, she heard, "Open it." Setting it on a nearby table, she untied the ribbon. Lifting the foil lid, she uncovered a five pound piece of chocolate fudge. Her stomach rebelled at the sight of it, and the aroma of the fine chocolate confection she had once considered heavenly now made her queasy.

Regardless, she forced an appreciative smile, holding it up for all to see. "I don't know how to thank you," she managed, and with a flash of inspiration, added, "except to offer you all a piece."

Her suggestion met with immediate and unanimous disapproval, whereupon she was informed that the candy was for *her* enjoyment. In addition, several employees made it clear they would not be satisfied until she had taken a taste.

Hoyt produced a knife, and cutting off a sizable chunk, offered it to her on the blade. Hiding the revulsion that could only be attributed to her previous, lengthy incident of indulgence, Lily bravely placed the gooey chocolate on her tongue, and facing the most challenging role she had ever played, she acted out her enjoyment as convincingly as possible, struggling to keep her smile from melting as quickly as the confection.

Swallowing the rich, creamy candy, she cleared her throat of the buttery residue. "Mackinac Island fudge is the greatest candy on earth, but your having given this to me makes it all the more special," she said sincerely. "I hope you will all have a good fall and winter. Thank you for being a part of my *Lily Belle* family, and if you want to sail with the Sweetwater Steamship Line next season, come back and see me in the spring."

Lily was deeply touched when many of her crew members made a special point to come to her before disembarking and tell her how much they had enjoyed their experiences aboard the *Lily Belle*. Some of the stewards and stewardesses were returning to colleges for fall classes and promised to apply for positions again in the spring. Others were experienced hands who had served previously with competing lines, and claimed her management was the best.

Before Lily left the dock, she asked Hoyt to meet with her the following morning to discuss the winter repair work he would oversee on the *Lily Belle*, for he would depart in two days to take her to her winter berth in Manitowoc.

Lily returned home quite fatigued from the Mackinac trip and expected to fall soundly asleep with island memories dancing in her mind. Instead, her thoughts kept straying to the departure of Hoyt and the *Lily Belle*, spreading a melancholy net over her. She had been so busy tending to the business of running a steamship line, she had given little consideration to the months between shipping seasons. Now they loomed before her like unscalable mountain cliffs.

Somehow, she must shore up her feelings, find new endeavors to which she could apply herself during the cold weather, and try not to think too often of Hoyt. To her dismay, she concluded that only the second of these three goals held real possibilities.

The following morning, Lily was not expecting Hoyt to

arrive in his elegant Cunningham carriage, but readily agreed to the suggestion of a drive in the country and luncheon at a favorite coach stop as their last outing before saying their good byes. Brilliantly clear blue skies promised abundant sunshine, and a temperate breeze blowing in off the lake made for a late summer day too fine for improvement.

Out on the open road, Hoyt drove his matched grays at a good clip for a short distance showing Lily their prowess, then slowed them to a comfortable trot for the remaining miles to an inn overlooking the Kalamazoo River. The keeper of the establishment knew Hoyt and seemed to be expecting them, showing them to a table with an excellent view.

The river was quite wide here, and evidently a favorite place for ducks and gulls, as well as small pleasure craft and fishing boats. The atmosphere was heavily laden with the tempting smell of freshly braised meat, and the cuisine was as pleasing as the view, featuring simply made American favorites such as steak, potatoes, and freshly baked rolls, followed by a choice of puddings—rice, tapioca, or vanilla.

Luncheon conversation remained comfortably free of references to their coming separation, centering instead on subjects closer at hand, such as the tastiness of their menu selections and the current of the river. When they had eaten their fill, Hoyt drove to a clearing upstream where they could walk along the bank, carrying with him a blanket which he threw down on a log.

Here, they talked for awhile about the refitting to be done on the *Lily Belle*, Hoyt making suggestions as to the work he considered necessary on a steamer that had seen but one season of service. Lily was glad for his advice and his experience.

166

"I know when you come sailing her into South Haven next spring, she'll look just like new," Lily concluded.

A cheerless look enhanced the droop of Hoyt's mustache and he reached for her hand, spreading it on his wide palm to stare down at its remarkably dainty size before closing his fingers around it. Looking into her oval face, slightly rounder now than when she had moved back to South Haven in July, he memorized once more the well marked brows forming a v above the brilliant sapphire of her eyes, the pert upturn at the end of her nose that often invited comment, the tiny dimple in the center of her well-shaped chin that deepened when she smiled.

It was barely perceptible now, for the woman staring into Hoyt's soulful brown eyes felt more like weeping than smiling as she waited patiently for him to say the words that his mouth was trying to form.

"I . . . I have something to ask you." Though he had made a rough beginning, he was determined to share his thoughts before the opportunity evaporated. "When your t . . . t . . . time draws near, if you want me to come, please give me plenty of notice. I don't go by t . . . t . . . train, and it takes a long while to go from Kewaunee to South Haven by buggy." He released her hand and turned away from the incredulous look that appeared as though it would erupt any moment in a torrent of questions.

CHAPTER

13

Though Lily could scarcely contain her curiosity, this time she had somehow grasped the concept of letting Hoyt do the talking in his own good time, rather than badgering him with questions that might make him even more uncomfortable than he obviously was already.

He was surprised when, after walking a few paces along the riverbank, Lily still had not spoken, and perhaps even more surprised at himself when he sat beside her again and muttled his way through as complete an explanation as he could manage of his dislike for travel by rail.

Starting with a description of his father, a brawny, often drunken engineer, and the terror wrought against him as a small boy, he gave chapter and verse of the ordeal he faced in his daily struggle with the resulting stammer, of the determination that developed within himself to avoid both alcohol and the rails, his pursuit of a career on the lakes that his father would have denied him. The circumstance had also prompted him to become owner of the finest horseflesh and carriage money could buy.

Lily remembered how the train in her third floor playroom had disturbed him, and now understood why. When she was certain Hoyt had said his piece, she reached out to him, lightly touching his bearded cheek. "Hoyt, I promise I'll give you lots of time to drive over from Kewaunee. Unless this rascal decides to fool both the doctor and me, you'll be here when he makes his debut." She pressed upward at the corner of his mouth, and he responded by favoring her with a smile.

His heart full, he ached to know if she had decided to

marry him when she was done mourning, but he realized this question would have to wait. He counted himself blessed knowing she wanted him there when her child was born.

The sun had barely made an appearance above the horizon the following morning when the *Lily Belle* steamed out of South Haven. Lily watched from her bedroom window as the vessel cleared the light on the south pierhead and turned north against four foot blue-gray waves, clouds of smoke trailing to a wisp in the overcast sky. She felt as though a very big part of her was now a vast, empty cavern, and had no notion of how to replenish it. The remaining weeks of September, and the months of October, November, December, and January stretched endless before her.

A stirring in Lily's womb turned her attention from the lakeshore scenario, and she lowered herself to her desk chair, her hand spanning her abdomen. For the first time, she felt her baby quickening within her. The milestone brought mixed feelings. On the most basic level, it enhanced within her the maternal instincts natural to a woman of her condition, giving a confirmation of the tiny infant that would in several months time become a real and demanding part of her life.

On a more practical level, she realized she was not certain even now that she would ever be prepared to face the challenge of raising Parker's child. She was pleased Agatha and Jack had decided to remain with her in South Haven throughout the winter. She could always count on her aunt for an encouraging word, though Agatha had never borne children of her own, and on Jack for practical, sound advice, though his parental experience had been cut tragically short when his only child, a son, had drowned at the age of ten.

She had yet to face the physical demands attending the birth of a child. Thank goodness for Dr. Adams. He seemed to be worthy of her trust and respect, a kind and understanding physician to see her through the discomforts of labor, which she dreaded.

The weeks immediately following Hoyt's departure from South Haven were for him marked by seasonal changes. The remaining days of September brought a range of weather conditions from the bright blues of fair skies and calm waters, to the grays and greens of the cooling and more turbulent, rainswept lake. Though in years past he had found solace in working on a nearby dairy farm, putting up silage and filling corn cribs for the winter season, the hard tasks of daily labor could not blot out the loneliness, apart from Lily.

Bates, the chief engineer of the *Lily Belle*, was by definition responsible for her maintenance. Conveniently, he resided in Manitowoc where repairs were being made. The town lay some thirty miles south of Hoyt's Kewaunee home, and he made weekly treks there to check on progress hoping to assuage his yearning to be with the ship's owner, but these excursions only made matters worse. Never before had he known such an ache in his soul.

The highlight of Lily's week was always the day on which the postman delivered news from Hoyt. His letters began in an almost terse style, describing the work that had been accomplished on her ship at Manitowoc. In contrast, they ended with several paragraphs related to his agricultural activities, and a few lines of tender assurance that he was thinking of her and praying for her good health.

For Lily, time was marked by the physical changes in

herself. By the end of October, her abdomen had grown much rounder, yet the child within often reminded her of its cramped quarters by seemingly trying to kick out the walls.

As Thanksgiving neared, Lily's family made plans to join her from back East, realizing travel for a woman in her condition could be difficult, uncomfortable, and possibly even risky. Though she enjoyed her reunion with her parents and older brother, she was not sorry to see them return to New York City, taking with them their scorn for small Midwestern ports, nor was she particularly sad to learn that their plans to spend Christmas in Europe would preclude a similar reunion the following month.

With the fall holiday behind her and Christmas fast approaching, Lily decided to make it a memorable event. Not only would it be the first time for celebrating in her very own home, but she had not shared this holiday with her aunt for many years. From the Montgomery Ward Catalog Lily ordered ribbons of satin and velvet, lace edgings, insertings, and trimmings, and colored moire antique yard goods in lavender, old rose, and pink, to satisfy Agatha's penchant for everything mauve. She ordered dozens of velvet and silk roses in buds, and half-blown and full-blown blossoms.

When the goods arrived, Agatha and Lily set their hands to the task of creating decorations for the tree they would put up in the parlor on Christmas Eve, for the mantle there and the bookshelves in the library office, and of course, for the front door.

Lily ordered Hoyt's gift from her favorite apothecary in New York, Caswell-Massey. She chose men's cologne, called George Washington No. Six, from the authentic recipe for the scent which had been worn by the historic personage, and had a crystal decanter with an engraved silver label shipped directly to Hoyt in Wisconsin.

Late in the afternoon on the day before Christmas, Jack and Ridgley managed to erect a perfectly shaped, seven-foot tall blue spruce in the front parlor window. Climbing a step ladder, Ridgley topped the tree with the angel Lily had fashioned from a doll's head and yards of white lace. With instructions from Lily and Agatha, the butler managed to decorate the upper branches with lacy confections, and happily left the lower boughs to their deft hands. A fireplace fire and bowl of wassail spiced with cinnamon and clove warmed the atmosphere nicely as the evergreen took on its new look.

Christmas Day brought the exchange of traditional gifts: suspenders, socks, and handkerchiefs for the men, and boxes of sweets for the ladies. In addition, Lily received from Hoyt a ten-pound round of aged extra-sharp cheddar cheese made from the milk of the dairy herd on the farm where he worked. How Lily wished he had come with the cheese on the train to South Haven for the holiday celebration.

With January came not only the start of a new year, but the first of the truly blustery weather that could blow in off the lake, dumping several inches of snow along the shoreline. Just as the bad weather settled in, a depression cast a dark shroud over Lily's spirits. Short daylight hours and heavy, gray clouds seemed destined to keep her in a sullen mood during the first week of January. Of no help at all was the fact that by now, her figure had ballooned to such a size that she could barely recognize her own chubby face in the mirror.

Still, she must endure four more weeks of pregnancy. How she longed for the day when Hoyt would arrive. She would send for him in about three week's time, allowing him several days to travel by coach.

By now, the baby was pressing against her rib cage causing such difficulty with respiration that she could barely make it to the top of the stairs without panting, and sleep had become difficult since she was unable to discover any prone position which was comfortable. Additionally, her back never seemed to stop aching, and her stomach often felt woozy.

Her feet and ankles swelled enough to render inconsequential the fact that she could no longer see them to don shoes. They remained in her closet while Agatha's hand knitted foot warmers kept her toes from succumbing to the wintry chill that pervaded every room.

Despite the inconveniences of her condition and the necessity of borrowing an oversize pair of boots from Jack to accommodate her bloated ankles, Lily made an effort to step outside and breathe fresh air at least once each day. Dr. Adams had impressed upon her the importance of exercising to keep strong, and she would not relinquish the dubious pleasure of filling her lungs with bracing winter air. Ridgley was meticulous in his work to keep her walkway free of snow, so her path was unhampered at least as far as the neighboring sidewalk.

After a week of glum, messy weather, Lily was eager to be outdoors in the glorious rays that glistened more brightly than ever off the blanket of white covering streets and yards, rooftops and fence posts. Agatha happened to come upon her in the back room as she was pulling on Jack's boots.

"Watch your step, now, dear. Ridgley says that beyond our driveway, the walks are still quite treacherous."

"You needn't worry. I'll be careful," Lily promised, wrapping a muffler about her neck and pulling it up to cover her mouth and nose.

The day was as cold as it was bright, the chilly air nip-

173

ping at the exposed skin of her forehead, but the winds had calmed, giving the whole outdoors the appearance of a storybook winter village. Indeed, beyond her own front walk, the street remained drifted, much to the delight of the children sledding down the St. Joseph Street hill.

Lily traveled in semi-circles about her own driveway for a few minutes, but the childlike remembrances of tromping through snow knee deep enticed her to venture farther. Cautiously, she followed a path cut by children who had dragged a sled behind. Once beyond the next door neighbor's house, she was determined to make it to the end of the street.

She took slow, careful steps, slogging along in the boots that swam on even her swollen feet, and had turned toward home when for reasons unknown, she started to lose her balance. Arms flailing, she tried desperately to stay upright, but landed gently on a deep, soft drift. Believing herself unharmed, she laughed out loud, brushed herself off, and continued toward home, but by the time she arrived, she experienced an alarming new sensation.

Repairing as swiftly as possible to her bedroom, she rapidly shed her heavy clothing, then lay down. A shiver trembled through her, then a mild, cramplike pain in the small of her back.

Margaret, who would serve as her monthly nurse, attending her and the baby during the first four weeks following delivery, had seen her come in, and must have sensed something was wrong, for within moments she was by Lily's side.

She listened to a description of the near fall and the back pain that had already disappeared, and ordered, "Lie perfectly still. I'll send Ridgley for Dr. Adams."

Both Agatha and Margaret came to sit with her while

174

waiting for the doctor. Lily had experienced two more pains at fifteen-minute intervals by the time he arrived.

Completing his examination, Dr. Adams gave his prognosis. "I have every reason to believe you're going to be a mother sooner than we thought."

"How soon?" Lily asked, thinking of the time Hoyt would require to travel from Wisconsin.

"It's hard to say, exactly. You might not deliver for another fifteen or sixteen hours."

"I'll send word to Hoyt," said Agatha, as if reading her niece's mind.

Lily was too preoccupied with the onslaught of another pain to explain that Agatha might as well wait until the baby was born to contact the captain, since he wouldn't be able to arrive in time for the delivery, anyhow.

The realization that Hoyt would not be with her made her intervals between cramps nearly as difficult to endure as the labor pains themselves. Lily silently chastised herself for getting into another predicament, then concluded that she could probably never change her impetuous nature. Nevertheless, she wasn't sure she could forgive herself if her own foolishness should prove harmful to her baby.

LILY FELL. BABY COMING.

Those four words constituting Agatha Atwood's telegram were enough to set Hoyt off in the direction of the train station, sans luggage. Though he had not been aboard a train since the day his father died, he marched with conviction up to the ticket agent and purchased one-way fare from Kewaunee to South Haven.

Fortunately he hadn't long to wait for departure. Within moments the Kewaunee, Green Bay, and Western Railroad's

175

iron horse came screeching to a halt at the platform. Only when he boarded did his fears and dreads surface anew.

The sight and stench of chewed tobacco in and around the spitoons gave rise to the nauseous feeling he had known in childhood. He settled onto a seat in first class, its brown plush worn from the armrests, its stained antimassacar long overdue to be changed. Across the aisle, an old codger cleared phlegm from his throat, rolled down his window and spat, then relit his fat cigar and began emitting huge, fetid puffs of smoke.

Hoyt considered moving, but gave up the notion. Only three empty seats remained. One faced his own. The second was forward, adjacent to a dandy who toted a liquor bottle wrapped none too discreetly in brown paper. The third would pair him with a woman whose flamboyant red cape and similarly colored hair made him question her reputation, and he would not risk the chance that unwanted familiarities could accompany passages through dark tunnels.

With a blast from the steam whistle, the train pulled away from the station, clacking its way down the track with a steadily increasing rhythm, a speed that seemed to set his own pulse to racing. Though he had shed his bulky woolen overcoat, beads of sweat soon trickled from his forehead.

He mopped his face with his handkerchief and reclined in his seat, but his effort to relax made matters worse, and though the train traveled down a perfectly straight track, he felt as though he were spinning.

As fence rails sped past, he tried to tell himself his urgent desire to get off and hire a buggy would pass, and that in no time he would be switching in Green Bay for the Chicago-bound train, but rational and logical thoughts could not overcome irrational emotions.

Nor could thoughts of Lily in labor distract him from the pain that seized the left side of his chest. He felt as though steel bands were constricting his heart, making breathing nearly impossible, but when he told himself to relax, the iron fingers only curled tighter.

After eight hours, Lily's contractions were still quite mild and not much closer together. She wanted desperately to get out of bed and stretch her legs, but Margaret wouldn't allow it.

"You've stopped bleedin' for the present, Mrs. Haynes," she said, upon examining her patient for what Lily thought must have been the hundredth time. "You should count yourself lucky for that, and be content to rest. 'Tis certain you'll need your strength later on. Standin' up and walkin' about now 'd only start the flow again, and that'd be a dangerous thing."

Lily grumbled.

Agatha, who hadn't left Lily's room since sending Ridgley to the telegraph office with the message for Hoyt, wagged her finger at her niece. "Now don't you be complaining to Margaret. You're lucky things aren't worse. If you like, I'll read to you."

Lily noted the volume of Franklin in her aunt's hands, and knew that she was in no frame of mind to hear repeated his thirteen virtues, of which Agatha seemed so fond. "Just help me to turn on my other side, then tell me some stories about the old days in Chicago," Lily requested.

With Agatha's and Margaret's help, she was soon situated as comfortably as possible in a new position. As Margaret hummed an Irish lullaby softly in the background, Agatha told about her days as a new bride in the Chicago of the late 1840's, when the town was still devoid of railroads.

177

The rumble down the tracks on which Hoyt rode, and the vastness of Union Station where his train screeched to a halt, was a far cry from the trackless, stationless town of Agatha's reminiscences.

Never had Hoyt been so relieved to step off a conveyance as he was to exit the passenger car in which he had been waging war with an invisible monster, and losing. He hurried down the platform into the station. His shirt was drenched with perspiration, and since he hadn't taken time to pack, he went straight to a men's shop where he purchased a fresh one, and a few toiletries.

His shopping spree, though brief, gave him some relief from the anxiety he had been experiencing on the train, but it also made him wonder whether he could face boarding the Michigan Central for the last leg of his journey.

He crossed to the opposite side of the cavernous, steel-beamed lobby to read the list of departures. In twenty minutes the South Haven train would pull out of the station. The fiber of every nerve told him he did not want to be on it.

At the nearby newspaper and periodical stand, he bought the latest issue of the *Chicago Tribune* and finding a bench near the platform of his Michigan Central connection, unfolded the paper before him, but he never even read the front page. In his mind raged a great debate.

Would he board this train? Of course! Lily needed him. He must employ the most expedient means possible to reach her. She was counting on him to be with her for the birth of her first child.

Droplets of moisture grew on his forehead, then a comforting inner voice told him, "It's too late. She'll already have given birth. No point in rushing. You might as well hire a rig at the livery and take your time."

His fluttering pulse settled into a steady beat as he folded his paper. Rising, he had stepped off in the direction of the Adams Street exit when the conductor barked, "Now boarding for Michigan City and points north: New Buffalo, Benton Harbor and St. Joe, South Haven—"

CHAPTER

14

Though the morning sun shone brightly in Lily's room, an unusual occurrence for Michigan in January, she barely noticed. Anxious as she was to be done with the birthing of her son, for she had been certain for several months that she was carrying a boy, Margaret now repeated the advice she had been giving her patient during the contractions that had come on during the past hour. "Breathe easy now, Mrs. Haynes. Don't push. It's not time yet. Save y'r strength."

Lily took short, shallow breaths, consciously attempting to heed the maid's warning, but frustration and overtiredness had done nothing to improve her mood of ten hours earlier. "It's not time yet . . . it's not time yet. You keep telling me it's not time yet. This baby's got to come soon. I'm already worn to a frazzle."

Agatha patted her niece's brow with a cool, damp cloth. "Dr. Adams said to fetch him when your pains are five minutes apart. Surely it won't be much longer now, dear."

"The babe 'll be here afore y' know it. It's time to ready y'r bed linens, Mrs. Haynes. You'll have to raise up some so I can fold y'r sheet back." Deftly, Margaret turned back the bottom sheet so it came no lower than Lily's waist, replacing it on the lower portion of the bed with an oil cloth topped by several layers of absorbent fabric. To the foot board, she affixed a long, twisted towel which Lily could grasp during the bearing-down pains yet to come.

All the while, Margaret hummed an Irish ditty. Between pains, Lily began trying to sing along with Margaret. The maid's repertoire of folk tunes from her native isle was quite extensive, and Lily found that concentration on learning the verses helped her to forget her discomfort.

The time for Dr. Adams's arrival came none too swiftly, and to Lily, the physician with his bulging black leather bag looked like a saint when he came through her door.

The recent heavy snows did nothing to hasten Hoyt's journey aboard the Michigan Central train bound for South Haven. Slowing at times to a mere twenty or twenty-five miles per hour, the engine cleared its track of tall drifts while the captain paced the length of his car, alternately wiping his brow and running his hand through his hair.

Two hours later than expected, the South Haven depot came into view. Hoyt nearly flew from the passenger car to the nearby livery. Tossing a five dollar gold piece to the only employee in sight, a youngster who had been charged with the responsibility of cleaning the stable and laying in a fresh supply of hay, Hoyt quickly learned which animal worked best in deep snow, and in record time, had fitted it with blanket and saddle and swung aboard.

Though tempted to dig his heels into the chestnut gelding's flanks, Hoyt reminded himself that road conditions rendered such action unwarranted, and reined in his own anxiety while the horse picked its way through drifts three feet high. Down River Street and Center, past the Sentinel Office and bank to Phoenix and Water Streets, he could think of nothing but Lily and the baby.

After a good bit of prancing through the abundant white fluff, Hoyt turned the corner onto Erie, and the gables of Lily's Queen Anne home at the end of the street came into view. Moments later, he was cranking the key of her front doorbell with one hand, while pounding on the oak door with the other. Ridgley ushered him in.

"Has she had the b . . . b . . . baby?" he asked, heedless of his bothersome stutter.

Ridgley helped him peel off his heavy coat. "No, sir. The doctor is with her, and so are Mrs. Wilson and Margaret. I'll tell them you're here."

Hoyt took a moment to remember Agatha was now properly referred to as Mrs. Wilson. Jack limped into the foyer to greet him. "Good to see you, son. Might as well join me in the front hall. I've got a nice fire going."

Hoyt jealously watched Ridgley ascend the stairs and debated whether to follow him to the second floor.

Jack must have read the mind of the man who had been like a son to him since his own boy had died. "The ladies wouldn't appreciate you getting in the way upstairs. There's nothing you can do but wait, and from what Doc Adams just told me, the waiting's almost over."

When the next pain hit, Lily braced her feet against the footboard, pulled on the towel Margaret had tied there, and bore down as hard as she could.

"Good, Mrs. Haynes. You're doing fine. The baby's coming now." Dr. Adams's soothing words gave her confidence.

In a breathless voice, Lily couldn't help asking, "Is it a boy?"

"We'll know soon. Save your breath now."

The onslaught of the next pain coincided with a knock on her bedroom door. Lily thought Agatha said something about Hoyt arriving, but she couldn't make sense of it. All of her concentration centered now on her delivery, and at the peak of the next powerful contraction, her infant made full entry into the world with a cry from healthy lungs.

"Congratulations, Mrs. Haynes. You're the mother of a healthy child!" announced Dr. Adams, laying the slippery babe in the cloth Margaret provided.

Lily lay panting for a few seconds, catching her breath. Her son was healthy, the doctor had said. Maybe she could rest now.

"Yessiree! Don't know when I've brought a prettier little girl into the world! Daresay she looks like her mother, too—"

"Girl?" she asked, too breathless to inquire how this could be when she was so certain only a son could have kicked up such a fuss during the last few weeks of her pregnancy.

"Definitely a daughter," the doctor confirmed, adding with a chuckle, "I would have known that even without medical training."

Agatha mopped her niece's brow. "She's a beautiful, petite little thing." She dropped the cloth into the washbasin. "I'll go downstairs and tell Hoyt. He'll be so pleased!"

Her aunt was gone before Lily found the energy to ask, "Am I imagining things, or did Auntie say Hoyt was downstairs?"

Margaret lay the infant beside her mother. "Aye. Captain Curtiss arrived only moments before your little miss made her appearance."

Hoyt had followed Jack into the front hall, but had yet to make contact with the seat of a chair. He had paced the floor in front of the fireplace, caught a glimpse of his tousled hair, rumpled shirt, and shadowed chin in the mirror above the mantle, then changed his route so he wouldn't have to look at himself.

Hearing the cry of an infant, he took up a post at the bottom of the stairs to wait for someone to come down with news. The clunk of a cane in the upstairs hallway was his assurance that within moments, Agatha would appear. The old lady soon began her unsteady descent, and he rushed up the steps to assist her.

She fixed him with her eagle eye. "Well, Captain, it wouldn't take a Harvard scholar to realize you're all at sea. Chipper up. Mother and baby daughter are both doing fine."

"C . . . C . . . Can I see them?" His words came stumbling out, but he was too preoccupied with concern for Lily to slow his tongue.

Agatha chuckled, not unkindly. "Give her a little while to rest and make herself presentable. She'll send for you when she's ready. In the meantime, I'll have Ridgley serve tea. You look like you need something to calm your nerves."

Hoyt never would have doubted Agatha's words, nor those of the doctor who on his departure, declared mother and baby in fine condition. Nevertheless, the captain wouldn't be satisfied about Lily's condition until he saw for himself.

For the next four hours, he felt as though he were sitting on the anxious seat. Too jittery for a full meal, he sipped tea, munched on common crackers, and browsed in the library until Margaret at last took him upstairs.

Lily was propped up in bed, lounging against a snowy drift of feather pillows, a coverlet tucked in about the waist. She wore a white bed jacket embroidered on its round collar with pink floss.

Her sweet, welcoming smile didn't hide the fatigue evident in the tiny lines about her eyes. Her pale yellow hair had been pulled back, twisted atop her head and tied up with a pink ribbon. She made a charming picture with her infant cradled in her arms.

Lily didn't realize how much she had missed Hoyt, nor

how his arrival would comfort her, until he stepped through her door. His dark, collar-length hair, always neat in the past, looked as though the only comb it had seen was his fingers. The generous mouth that curled naturally upward at the corners was set in a tight, rigid line, and the mustache above that had heretofore been perfectly groomed, had obviously been mussed by nervous fingers.

He was still as fit as when she had last seen him though, for despite a rumpled waistcoat, the familiar wide, rugged shoulders and firm chest tapered to a still narrow waist and hips, of which she could be envious.

"I'm glad you're here," Lily said softly, not wanting to wake the baby. She pulled back the flannel blanket. "What do you think of her?"

Hoyt wasn't certain what he had expected, but certainly not the blotchy red infant harbored in Lily's arms. He took a second to remind himself this was the reason he had come all the way from Kewaunee by train, and that Lily was watching his reaction closely. He noticed the tiny little fist with the remarkably perfect fingers and nails. Gingerly, he stroked the back of the baby's hand. Even in her sleep, the infant grasped his little finger, and as she curled her own about it, she claimed his heart as well.

A warmth spread all through him. Until now, Hoyt would not have believed the disproportionate effect such a small gesture could have on him. "She's got quite a grip on me," he said in a shaky whisper. He released his hand and stroked the peach fuzz on her scalp. "May . . . I hold her?"

Hoyt cradled the sleeping infant in arms that suddenly seemed overly large and uncoordinated. Shifting the small bundle slightly, he noted how feather-light she felt, how perfect her tiny features. Stunned to silence, he lifted his head and met Lily's searching gaze.

185

His tongue had never felt more free, yet only his eyes carried his eloquent message. *This child, while not born of our love, binds you and me, Lily. I'll help you raise her. I'll love her like my own . . . if you'll marry me.*

The sight of the rugged man, hunching his broad shoulders to nestle the babe, brought a lump to Lily's throat. *Oh, Hoyt,* she answered him, the thought so vibrant and palpable that it needed no words, *what a father you'd make for little Agatha Katherine! But the mourning period . . . it wouldn't be proper.* Only a small doubt remained, quickly dislodged by her overpowering love for him. *Oh, yes, yes! I'll marry you if you'll wait for us!*

I'd wait for you forever, Lily! And I'll even give up sailing on Lake Michigan if it would please you—

Oh, Hoyt, I'd never ask you to give up the lake. It's your life!

You're first with me, Lily—you and the baby. Nothing else on earth comes close to what I'm feeling right now—

All this—without a word passing between them—so electrified the atmosphere that each was riveted to the spot, hardly daring to breathe lest the spell be broken. They drank in the moment, making endless promises, pledging lasting love.

There would be time—sun-dappled days and moon-soft nights—to get to know each other, the three of them. Yes, there would be lots of time.

THE END

MORE ABOUT GREAT LAKES SHIPPING
The following books provide excellent information:
Ships of the Great Lakes by James P. Barry
Ladies of the Lakes by James Clary
FICTION INSPIRED BY HISTORICAL EVENTS
On June 4, 1901, a highly publicized steamship race between the *City of Erie* and the *Tashmoo* was run on Lake Erie. This piece of history provided inspiration for *The Captain and the Widow*.
ABOUT DONNA WINTERS
Donna adopted Michigan as her home state in 1971 when she moved there from a small town outside of Rochester, New York. She began penning novels in 1982 while working full time for Lear/Siegler, Inc. (now Smiths Industries), of Grand Rapids. She resigned in 1984 following a contract offer for her first book. Since then, she has written five romance novels for various publishers including Thomas Nelson Publishers and Zondervan Publishing House.

Her husband, Fred, an American History teacher, shares her enthusiasm for history. Together, they visit historical sites, restored villages, museums, and lake ports, taking camera and tape recorder to capture a slice of America's past which she can share with her readers and he with his students.

Donna spent the summers of her youth at her parents' cottage on Lake Ontario, and has always lived in states bordering on the Great Lakes. Her familiarity and fascination with these remarkable inland waters and her residence in the heart of Great Lakes Country make her the perfect candidate for writing *Great Lakes Romances*$_{TM}$.

MACKINAC
First in the series of *Great Lakes Romances*^{tm}

Her name bespoke the age in which she lived . . .
But **Victoria Whitmore** was no shy, retiring Victorian
miss. Never a homebody, attending to the whims of her
cabinetmaker Papa, she found herself aboard the *Algomah*,
traveling from staid Grand Rapids to Michigan's fashionable
Mackinac Island resort.

Her journey was not one of pleasure; a restful holiday
did not await her. Mackinac's Grand Hotel owed the
Whitmores money—enough to save the furniture manufacto-
ry from certain financial ruin. It became Victoria's mission
to venture to the island to collect the payment. At Mackinac, however, her task was anything but easy, and she found
more than she had bargained for.

Rand Bartlett, the hotel manager, was part of that
bargain. Accustomed to challenges and bent on making the
struggling Grand a success, he had not counted on the challenge of Victoria—and he certainly had not counted on
losing his heart to her.

(Note: Lily, the heroine of The Captain and the Widow, *is
an important secondary character in* Mackinac.*)*

ORDER FORM

Customer Name

Address

Available while supplies last.

Quantity		Total	
	The Captain and the Widow, $6.95		
	Mackinac, $6.95		
	Subtotal:		
	Michigan residents include 4% tax:		
	Postage - add $1 for first item, 50¢ for each additional:		
	Total:		

Send check or money order to:
Bigwater Publishing
Order Department
P.O. Box 177
Caledonia, MI 49316

READER SURVEY—*THE CAPTAIN AND THE WIDOW*

Your opinion counts! Please fill out and mail this form to:
Reader Survey   Your Name:
Bigwater Publishing   Address:
P.O. Box 177   (optional)
Caledonia, MI 49316

If you include your name and address, we will send you a bookmark and
the latest issue of our *Great Lakes Romances*_{TM} *Newsletter*.

1. Please rate the following elements from 1 (poor) to 5 (excellent):

_____Heroine   _____Hero   _____Setting   _____Plot

Comments:_____

_____

2. What setting (time and place) would you like to see in a future book?

_____

3. Where did you purchase this book?

_____

4. What influenced your decision to purchase this book?

_____Publicity (Please describe)_____

_____

_____Front Cover   _____First Page   _____Back Cover Copy

_____Title   _____Friends   _____Other (please describe)_____

5. Please indicate your age range:

_____Under 18   _____25-34   _____46-55

_____18-24   _____35-45   _____Over 55